Party Animals

"Isn't this great, Elizabeth? I'm having so much—yuck!" Jessica lifted her foot off the floor. Her shoe was covered with grape soda.

Someone in the living room turned up the stereo about three times louder than it had been before. The walls were shaking from the noise. "I hope the neighbors can't hear this!" Elizabeth said.

"Hey, get out of there!" Jessica yelled at a boy who was taking a package of cookies out of the cupboard. He ignored her and took the bag into the living room.

Elizabeth looked around the kitchen. It was a total mess. There were half-full cups everywhere, and popcorn was sprinkled on the floor like confetti. She picked up a cup from the floor and tossed it into the trash. "Jess, do you think maybe things are getting a little out of control?"

Elizabeth didn't hear Jessica's answer—it was drowned out by a loud crash from the living room.

Bantam Books in the SWEET VALLEY TWINS AND FRIENDS series
Ask your bookseller for the books you have missed

SWEET VALLEY TWINS
AND FRIENDS

The Big
Party
Weekend

Written by
Jamie Suzanne

Created by
FRANCINE PASCAL

A BANTAM SKYLARK BOOK
NEW YORK · TORONTO · LONDON · SYDNEY · AUCKLAND

RL 4, 008–012

THE BIG PARTY WEEKEND
A Bantam Skylark Book / November 1991

Sweet Valley High® and Sweet Valley Twins and Friends are
trademarks of Francine Pascal

Conceived by Francine Pascal

Produced by Daniel Weiss Associates, Inc.
33 West 17th Street
New York, NY 10011

Cover art by James Mathewuse

Skylark Books is a registered trademark of Bantam Books, a division of
Bantam Doubleday Dell Publishing Group, Inc.
Registered in U.S. Patent and Trademark Office and elsewhere.

ISBN 0-553-15952-6

Published simultaneously in the United States and Canada

Bantam Books are published by Bantam Books, a division of Bantam
Doubleday Dell Publishing Group, Inc. Its trademark, consisting of
the words "Bantam Books" and the portrayal of a rooster, is Registered
in U.S. Patent and Trademark Office and in other countries. Marca
Registrada. Bantam Books, 666 Fifth Avenue, New York, New York
10103.

PRINTED IN THE UNITED STATES OF AMERICA

OPM   0 9 8 7 6 5 4 3 2 1

The Big Party Weekend

One

◆

"I can't believe Mom and Dad are going to Mexico!" Jessica Wakefield said as she barged into her twin sister's room. "I can't wait until we're on our own."

Elizabeth looked puzzled. "What do you mean, Jessica?"

"They're going away for five days, right? And they told us where they're going and what they're going to do and all that," Jessica said. She stopped in front of Elizabeth's mirror to fix her hair. "But they didn't say one word about what *we* were going to do while they were gone."

Elizabeth shrugged. "The usual, probably. Go to school, do our homework—"

"No!" Jessica cried, interrupting her. "See, Mom and Dad didn't mention anything about us having a baby-sitter while they were gone. Don't you get it? We're going to be free!''

"I don't know, Jess. Do you really think they'd leave us all alone for five days? Anyway, even if they did, we still have to go to school."

"I know," Jessica said. "But we can stay up as late as we want and eat dinner whenever we want." She turned from the mirror and laughed. "It's going to be great!"

Elizabeth wasn't sure, at first. But the more she thought about it, the more she liked the idea of their parents trusting them enough to leave them on their own. Maybe now that she and Jessica were in sixth grade at Sweet Valley Middle School, they didn't need someone to look after them.

Elizabeth smiled at her twin. Jessica and Elizabeth looked like mirror images on the outside, with their identical long blond hair and blue-green eyes, but they were complete opposites on the inside. Jessica was a member of the Unicorns, a club of pretty and popular girls who spent most of their time talking about clothes and boys. Jessica liked to live for the moment, and when she wanted to do something, she did it—and thought about the consequences later.

Elizabeth took her responsibilities seriously. She spent most of her free time working on *The Sweet Valley Sixers,* her class's weekly newspaper. She also enjoyed hanging out with close friends and, more recently, spending time with Todd Wil-

kins. Even though the twins had different person-
alities and interests, they had always been best
friends, and they knew they always would be.

"Maybe Mom and Dad just haven't found a
baby-sitter yet," Elizabeth said, sitting down at
her desk. "Maybe that's why they didn't say
anything."

"Elizabeth, it's Sunday and they're leaving
Wednesday. They won't have time to find one,
even if they did want to," Jessica said. "After they
leave, we'll have the whole house to ourselves. I
can't wait!"

Elizabeth looked suspiciously at her sister.
"What are you planning?"

"Oh, nothing," Jessica said. "Yet!"

On Monday morning, Jessica could hardly
keep her mind on her social studies class. She
couldn't wait to surprise everyone at lunch with
her big news. She hadn't told her best friend, Lila
Fowler, about it when she talked to her on Sunday
night. She hadn't even told her own sister what
she was planning yet.

When the bell rang, Jessica rushed out of the
classroom and down the hall to the cafeteria.
When she walked in, though, she tried to act completely casual. A few of her friends were already
sitting at their usual table, which they called the
Unicorner.

"Hi, Jessica," Ellen Riteman said when Jessica sat down beside her. "How was your weekend?"

"Fantastic," Jessica said.

"Really? What did you do?" Janet Howell, president of the Unicorns, asked.

"Well, not too much. But I found out something you're not going to believe," Jessica said.

Lila looked skeptical. "What?"

"This weekend is going to go down in history as one of the best weekends ever," Jessica declared. She glanced around the table at everyone.

"Well?" Tamara Chase prodded. "What did you want to tell us?"

"My parents are going to Mexico for five days, and I'm having a huge party on Saturday night."

"Your baby-sitter's going to let you have a party?" Ellen asked.

"Nope," Jessica said smugly.

"Then how are you going to get away with it?" Tamara asked.

"Simple. We don't *have* a baby-sitter," Jessica said triumphantly. "My parents are leaving us all alone for five days."

"You're kidding," Lila said.

"No, I'm not," Jessica said. "I guess they think we're old enough to stay by ourselves. So the first thing I decided was that I'd have a party while they're gone."

"That is so cool," Ellen said. "I wish my parents would go on vacation and leave me home alone. But then I'd have to take care of my little brother, so I guess it wouldn't be so great."

"So, who are you inviting?" Janet asked.

"Oh, everybody," Jessica said. "I mean, everybody that we'd want to be there."

"I'll ask some people, if you want," Janet offered.

"OK. Can everybody come on Saturday night, around seven?" Jessica asked.

Everyone at the table said "yes" enthusiastically, and Jessica felt incredibly grown-up. As far as she knew, no one in their grade had thrown a party without parents before. She loved being a trend-setter.

Just then, she had a great idea. "I'll be right back," she told everyone at the table.

She stepped into the lunch line next to Aaron Dallas. "Hi, Aaron," she said. "I'm having a party Saturday night. Can you come?"

He smiled at her. "This Saturday? Sure, I guess so."

This is going to be great! Jessica thought.

"Elizabeth, wait up!"

Elizabeth turned around and saw Jessica running toward her. It was the end of the day, and everyone was streaming out of Sweet Valley Middle School.

"I have something important to tell you," Jessica said when she caught up to her sister. "I had this great idea today—"

Before Jessica could say another word, Aaron, Ken Matthews, and Tom McKay rode up beside the twins on their bikes. "Hey, Jessica, you didn't tell us what time to show up Saturday night," Ken said.

Elizabeth stared at Jessica. "What's going on Saturday night?"

"Good one, Elizabeth," Tom said, laughing.

"Seriously, what time does the party start?" Aaron asked.

"Around seven," Jessica answered.

"OK, we'll be there," Ken said as they started to ride away.

"Don't be late!" Jessica called out after them. She turned to Elizabeth. "Did you see the way Aaron looked at me? He definitely likes me."

"Jessica, what party are you talking about?" Elizabeth asked suspiciously.

"That's what I was going to tell you. We're having a party this weekend!" Jessica announced with a grin.

"Do you really think it's a good idea to have a party while Mom and Dad are away?" Elizabeth asked.

"It's not a good idea, it's a terrific idea," Jessica answered.

"I don't know," Elizabeth said. "Did you ask Mom and Dad?"

Jessica shook her head. "Of course not! They'd never say yes."

"But you're going to do it anyway?"

"Sure. It's no big deal. If it'll make you feel better, we can tell them we're going to have a few friends over while they're gone," Jessica said.

"I don't think we should have a big party without asking them first," Elizabeth argued.

"Don't be such a party pooper!" Jessica said. "This is the first time we've ever had the house all to ourselves. We *have* to take advantage of it."

"But if we have a big party and they find out about it—"

"How are they going to find out about it?" Jessica interrupted. "They'll be hundreds of miles away. Come on, Elizabeth, it'll be fun. You can ask Amy and Julie and Todd—and whoever else you want to. *Please* don't tell Mom and Dad about it, pretty please?" Jessica begged.

"Well, OK," Elizabeth agreed. "I won't say anything. But we're going to have to be careful."

"Don't worry. Nothing bad will happen. I promise."

Two

◇

"I told you we weren't going to have a baby-sitter," Jessica said after dinner on Monday. She flopped onto Elizabeth's bed. "They still haven't said anything about it, so it's definite."

"It looks that way," Elizabeth agreed. "I'm glad they decided to trust us. I mean, we are almost thirteen."

Jessica heard heavy footsteps on the stairs, and a few seconds later the twins' fourteen-year-old brother, Steven, stepped into the room and closed the door behind him. "This is confidential," he said. "I'm having a party here on Saturday, and I don't want you guys in the way."

"You're planning a party for Saturday night?" Jessica asked, jumping up excitedly. "This is perfect! I'm having a party then, too. I mean, Elizabeth and I are both having it."

"You are?" Steven's eyes widened. "But I

already made plans," he protested. "I've invited people and everything."

"Well, so did I," Jessica said. "And I have the perfect solution—let's combine our parties!"

"Are you serious?" Steven asked.

Jessica nodded. Normally she tried to stay as far away as possible from Steven and his obnoxious friends, unless one of them was cute. But if her party was for high school kids, too, it would be even cooler. "We can go in together on stuff like chips and soda. It'll be cheaper, and it's not like there's not enough room for everybody."

"Steven, are you sure we're not going to have a baby-sitter?" Elizabeth asked.

"Of course we're not!" Steven replied. "They haven't said one word about it, and they're leaving the day after tomorrow. We're going to have the place to ourselves. It's going to be awesome. I don't know about this joint party, though."

"Come on, Steven, it'll be fun," Jessica said.

Steven thought it over for a minute. "I guess it'll be OK. But you have to promise that you and your silly friends won't bug my friends," he said.

Jessica glared at her brother. "They're not silly, and we won't bug you if you don't bug us."

"Deal," Steven agreed.

"The first thing we have to do is figure out how we're going to come up with the money to buy food and stuff," Jessica said.

"Can't we just raid the cabinets?" Steven asked.

"Knowing your friends, there probably isn't enough food in the house to feed them," Elizabeth said.

Steven nodded. "True."

"Yeah, and we want good food, not green beans and stuff," Jessica added. "We should have potato chips, tortilla chips, salsa, dip, maybe some taco salad, ice cream—"

"It's a party, not a five-course meal," Steven pointed out.

"Steven's right, we don't have to have everything," Elizabeth said. "Just the basic munchies." She got her wallet out of her knapsack. "I can contribute five dollars, but that's it."

"I have a couple of dollars, but they're in penny rolls, and I have to cash them in," Steven said.

"That's not enough," Jessica complained.

"Well, what do *you* have?" Steven countered.

Jessica thought for a moment. At her last count, she was fourteen dollars and fifty cents in debt. "I have the new Johnny Buck tape," she said, finally.

"That's what I thought," Steven said. "So where are we going to get the money for this thing? We can't exactly ask Mom and Dad for it."

"We could ask people to bring food," Elizabeth suggested.

"No way!" Jessica said vehemently. "If we're going to give a party, we have to do it right."

"Maybe Mom and Dad will give us some extra money for when they're gone, you know, to order pizzas for dinner," Steven said hopefully.

"Yeah, that would work," Jessica said. If it didn't, she would have to think of something else. She had told all of the Unicorns that her party was going to be the best ever, and she had invited almost everyone she knew. If her party wasn't a hit, she would be totally humiliated.

"Good morning," Elizabeth said to Steven and her parents as she sat down at the breakfast table on Tuesday. Jessica was still upstairs, getting ready for school.

"Good morning," Mr. Wakefield said.

Elizabeth helped herself to a glass of orange juice and poured some cereal into a bowl. "Dad, Mom, is there anything you want us to do around the house while you're gone? Something to keep us busy maybe?" Elizabeth had decided she wanted to do something nice for her parents. That way she wouldn't feel so bad about having the party while they were gone.

Steven looked at Elizabeth as if she were crazy.

"I can't think of anything right off the top of my head," Mrs. Wakefield said.

"I can," Mr. Wakefield said. He took a sip of coffee. "But it's a pretty big project."

"What is it?" Elizabeth asked.

"Well, there's so much junk piled up in the garage, it's impossible to find anything. I was looking for a rake the other day, and I almost got buried by an avalanche of old clothing."

"There is a lot of old stuff in there," Mrs. Wakefield agreed. "We haven't cleaned it in years. I think your old tricycles are still in there and about two dozen old board games."

"We'd love it if you could pick the place up a little. Make neat piles of things and then we can—"

"Have a garage sale!" Steven suddenly interrupted.

"I guess we could do that," Mr. Wakefield said. "But I was thinking we could donate all of the things that are in good shape to charity."

"I have an idea," Steven said, tapping his knife against his plate. "If we do all the work for the garage sale, how about if we donate half the money we make to charity—and keep the other half for ourselves?"

"Hmm," Mrs. Wakefield said. "That seems fair. Do you want to do it while we're gone?"

"Oh, definitely!" Steven said quickly. Elizabeth knew what he was so excited about—they'd be able to raise some money for their party. "I mean, that way it'll be clean when you come back," he added.

"Then it's settled," Mr. Wakefield said.

"What's settled?" Jessica asked as she walked into the kitchen.

"We're having a garage sale this week, to clean out the garage while Mom and Dad are gone," Steven told her.

Jessica frowned. "We are?"

"Yeah, we're going to donate half the proceeds to charity and keep the other half," Steven explained with a smile.

"Oh," Jessica said. Then a few seconds later she added, "That sounds like fun!"

Mr. and Mrs. Wakefield laughed as Jessica sat down at the table. "That's the first time I've ever heard you call work fun, Jessica," Mrs. Wakefield observed.

Jessica filled her bowl with cereal. "It just seems like a fun way to make some money," she said. "I mean, for a good cause and all."

Elizabeth took a sip of orange juice to keep from laughing. Then she stood up and picked up her knapsack.

Jessica quickly finished her cereal, and she and Steven followed Elizabeth out the door. "Bye!" Jessica cheerfully called over her shoulder to her parents. When the door closed, she grabbed Elizabeth's arm and started skipping down the sidewalk. "I knew we'd think of something!"

"We'd think of something?" Elizabeth repeated. "It was my idea."

"This is going to be great," Steven said, following them down the sidewalk. "Maybe we'll even have some money left over. You're a genius, Elizabeth."

"Actually, I wasn't thinking about the party," Elizabeth said, "but I guess this could solve our money problems. When should we have the sale?"

"How about Saturday?" Steven suggested.

"No, it can't be Saturday, we'll be too busy getting ready for the party," Jessica said.

"Then let's do it on Friday after school," Steven said.

"I can't do it then. I have a Unicorn meeting," Jessica said.

"Well, when do you want to do it?" Steven asked.

"Let's have it on Thursday afternoon. I'll make signs at school today on the photocopy machine and put them up around town."

"That's a start," Elizabeth said. "We'll have to spend this afternoon cleaning out the garage, and then tomorrow we can organize everything for the sale."

"The garage. Three-thirty. Be there," Steven said and headed for Sweet Valley High.

"Do you think it's going to work, having Steven's friends and our friends at the same party?" Elizabeth asked Jessica.

"Sure. Why wouldn't it?" Jessica said. "It's going to be the best party anyone at school's ever thrown. Trust me."

Jessica spent the first part of her lunch period in the library, photocopying the sign she'd made to advertise the garage sale. When she got to the cafeteria, everyone else was almost finished eating.

"Jessica, where have you been?" Lila asked when she sat down.

"I had to make these." Jessica held up one of her signs.

"You're having a garage sale?" Janet asked.

"We told my parents we'd do it while they're away, and they're going to let us keep the money," Jessica said. "We're going to use some of it for the party Saturday. You guys haven't forgotten about it, have you?"

"How could we, you keep reminding us every half hour," Lila mumbled.

"Guess what?" Jessica continued, ignoring Lila's comment. "My brother's inviting a bunch of kids from his class, too." She knew that would impress Janet, who was in the eighth grade. "We'll be like co-hosts."

"What about Elizabeth?" Mary Wallace, another Unicorn, asked.

"Oh, she'll be there, too," Jessica said. Across the cafeteria, she spotted Aaron, tossing a milk carton around with his friends. She had been thinking about him all day. He was so cute. Some people thought they were a couple, but they really weren't. Not yet, anyway. They had gone on a date to a Lakers' game once, but they had never kissed. If he kissed her at her very own party, that would be the best. Everyone was going to be there, and everyone would know that Aaron really liked her. She tried to picture what it would be like when she and Aaron finally kissed . . .

"Jessica. Earth to Jessica." Ellen Riteman was waving her hand in front of Jessica's face.

"What?" Jessica said, annoyed at the interruption.

"I asked if it's OK if I invite Rick?" Ellen said.

"Of course," Jessica said. "I have a feeling this could be a very romantic evening."

"Jessica, could you pass the salad?" Mr. Wakefield asked.

Jessica groaned as she lifted the wooden

bowl. "I don't know if I can. My arms are killing me."

"Mine don't feel so great either," Steven admitted. He rubbed his right shoulder. "There was a lot more stuff in the garage than I thought." They had spent a few hours before dinner on Tuesday moving things around, throwing out some things, and making neat piles of the junk they thought they could sell.

"Well, don't work too hard," Mrs. Wakefield said. "There's only so much the three of you can do."

"All that work made me twice as hungry," Elizabeth said, digging into her spaghetti.

"Then if Steven's twice as hungry as usual, we're in trouble," Mr. Wakefield joked.

Jessica speared a slice of tomato with her fork and was about to pop it into her mouth when her mother said, "Speaking of food, we want to let you know that you don't have to do all your own cooking while we're away."

"Great!" Steven said. "Can we get pizzas delivered every night?"

Mrs. Wakefield laughed. "No, that's not what we had in mind. We've hired someone to stay at the house, do the cooking and cleaning, and look after the three of you."

Jessica swallowed the tomato with a gulp. "Wh-what?"

"Her name is May Brown, and she comes very highly recommended by the Morrises. She's a nice, elderly woman and apparently a very good cook. I'm sure you won't be disappointed."

Mr. Wakefield was right. Jessica wasn't disappointed—she was crushed! They didn't come right out with the "B" word, but they were definitely talking about a baby-sitter! "Why do we need someone to stay here?" she asked. "We'll be fine on our own."

"Maybe you would, but we wouldn't feel comfortable leaving you by yourselves while we're so far away," Mrs. Wakefield said. "If we were only going to San Francisco, we might feel differently."

"So go to San Francisco," Jessica murmured under her breath.

"What's that?" Mr. Wakefield asked.

"Nothing," said Jessica. "Don't you think we're old enough to look after ourselves? Steven's in ninth grade, and Elizabeth and I are almost thirteen."

"And we know how to cook," Steven added.

"It's not just that," Mr. Wakefield said. "We want someone to be here in case there's an emergency. What if something happened to one of you? We'd never forgive ourselves if something went wrong."

"Nothing's going to go wrong," Elizabeth argued.

"Probably not, honey, but we won't be able to relax on our trip unless we know there's someone here to look after you," Mrs. Wakefield added. "Now, we know you're old enough to keep up with your responsibilities, like school. But we want someone here just in case. You can understand that, can't you?"

No, I can't! Jessica thought angrily. *How am I going to tell everyone at school that the party's been called off? And because we have a baby-sitter?*

"We promise we'll be really good and clean up and all that," Steven said in a final effort. "And I'll make sure Jessica and Elizabeth do their homework and go to sleep at the right time."

Jessica raised one eyebrow.

"Steven, we appreciate your offer, but we've made a decision," Mrs. Wakefield said. "Mrs. Brown will be here tomorrow when you get home from school—we'll be leaving right after breakfast. Now, I know you don't need to be told to have good manners, but please make her feel welcome."

Jessica sighed. *So much for hosting the bash of the year!*

Three

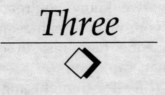

"Elizabeth, do me a favor," Jessica said as they walked to school the next morning. "Don't tell anyone the party is off yet."

"Why not?" Elizabeth asked. "We have to tell them sometime."

"I know," Jessica grumbled, kicking a pebble with her sneaker. "I want to think of a good excuse first. There's no way I can tell people the real reason we can't have the party. I'd be the laughingstock of the whole school!"

"It's not that bad," Elizabeth said. "People would understand."

She looked pleadingly at Elizabeth. "No, they wouldn't. Just promise, please!"

Elizabeth shrugged. "OK, I'll keep it a secret for today anyway."

"There's Lila. I'll see you later," Jessica said,

walking over to a group of Unicorns. "Hi, guys," she said. "What's up?"

"Nothing. We were just talking about your party," Kimberly Haver said. "It'll be so much fun to have your house to ourselves."

Jessica nodded.

"You look really tired. Are you all right?" Lila asked.

"I'm fine," Jessica replied with a smile, forcing herself to sound cheerful. The truth was, when she woke up that morning, she had felt even worse than she had the night before. She hadn't been able to fall asleep for a long time, and when she did, she dreamed that everyone in school was laughing at her and calling her a baby.

"How late do you think the party will go?" Ellen asked.

"Oh, I don't know," Jessica said with a shrug. "Pretty late, I guess." She decided she might as well keep talking up the party, until she came up with her excuse. "It'll probably go until midnight—you know Steven's friends."

"I'm glad we finally have a good weekend to look forward to," Janet said, flipping her hair over her shoulder. "There hasn't been a decent party around here since Aaron Dallas's and that seems like months ago."

Hearing Aaron's name made Jessica nervous

all over again. What would happen when *he* found out she wasn't as grown-up as she said she was? He might not want to go out with her after all. This was a disaster!

Elizabeth found her best friend, Amy Sutton, on the school steps a few minutes before the first bell. "Hi, Amy," she said, sitting down beside her.

"Hi, Elizabeth. I tried to call you last night, but the line was busy," Amy said.

"My mom was checking on all of their travel arrangements," Elizabeth explained.

"Aren't they leaving today?"

Elizabeth nodded. "They were going to drive to the airport in L.A. right after breakfast."

"Does it feel weird to be left on your own?" Amy asked.

Elizabeth shrugged. "Not really," she said. "Anyway, they'll be back soon."

"I was trying to call you last night because I asked my new boyfriend, Rob, to come to your party, and he said yes. Isn't that great?" Amy said.

"Did you say your *boyfriend*?" Elizabeth asked. As far as she knew, Amy didn't have a boyfriend, and it was obvious that she liked Ken Matthews.

"Yeah, I told you about him. He's the guy

I met at the mall last week. His name is Rob, and he's in eighth grade," Amy said. "He is *so* cute."

Elizabeth was so surprised she didn't know what to say. "I didn't know he was your boyfriend," she said. "Why didn't you tell me?"

"I guess I was kind of nervous about it," Amy said. "I mean, I didn't know if he liked me back. But I met him at the mall yesterday after school, and we hung out together for a while. That's when I asked him to your party. It is OK, isn't it?"

"Sure," Elizabeth said. It didn't matter who was invited to the party, as long as they didn't show up on Saturday night. "So what's he like?" she asked.

"He's really cute—"

"I got that part," Elizabeth said, laughing.

"OK, well, he's on the soccer team, and he's really good at video games—I watched him play a whole bunch yesterday at the mall," Amy explained. "Oh, and he's incredibly funny, too."

"He sounds nice," Elizabeth said. "But what about Ken? I thought he was going to be your first boyfriend."

"Sure, if I wanted to wait until I was eighty years old. Ken's more interested in football than me. Lately the only time he talks to me is when he wants to know how to do the math homework."

"Really? I thought you guys liked each other," Elizabeth said.

"Ken's nice and everything, but Rob is so much cooler," Amy said. "I can't wait for you to meet him. It's going to be great now that we both have boyfriends. I was thinking, maybe some day after school this week you, me, Todd and Rob could all go to Casey's for ice cream."

"That sounds like fun," Elizabeth said. "I'll ask Todd if he wants to, OK?"

"Great," Amy said. "I swear, Elizabeth, now I know why you got so nervous with Todd. I've never liked anyone this much before."

"I don't see why we have to go through with this dumb garage sale," Jessica complained when she met Elizabeth outside after school Wednesday afternoon. "It's not like we need the money for our party."

"We promised Mom and Dad that we'd do it for them," Elizabeth said. "We can't back out now."

"Well, we promised everyone we were having a party, and we're backing out of *that*," Jessica argued.

"That's different," Elizabeth said. "We probably shouldn't have planned to have a party without Mom and Dad's permission, anyway."

Jessica stared at her sister. "You sound like you're glad the party's off."

"No, I'm not," Elizabeth said. "I wanted to have the party, too. I just didn't want to go behind their backs."

"The next thing you're going to tell me is that you're glad some old lady is coming to stay with us," Jessica grumbled.

"Not really. But she is supposed to be really nice. I bet she's a lot like Grandma Wakefield. She'll make tons of cookies and brownies and get upset if we don't eat them all."

"I don't care if she can cook," Jessica said. "All the brownies in the world can't make up for ruining our party. And I don't want some stranger telling me what to do, either! We haven't had a baby-sitter for at least five years."

"I know," Elizabeth said. "I wish Mom and Dad trusted us enough to leave us by ourselves."

"It's *totally* humiliating," Jessica went on. "I mean, we're old enough to *be* baby-sitters. Can you imagine if anyone at school finds out about this?"

Elizabeth and Jessica turned to walk up their driveway. "Well, as long as she doesn't treat us like little kids, I guess it won't be so bad," Elizabeth said.

The first thing Elizabeth saw when she walked

into the kitchen was Steven, standing with his arms folded across his chest, glaring at a woman with gray hair and glasses—who was glaring right back at him. Was this May Brown, the nice, grandmotherly type who was going to be staying with them?

She turned to the twins, and her frown deepened. "It's about time you got home! Your parents told me the walk only took fifteen minutes," she said.

Jessica glanced at her watch. "We only got out of school twenty minutes ago. What's the big deal?"

"Which one are you?" Mrs. Brown asked, coming closer.

"Jessica. I guess you're Mrs. Brown," she said.

"Call me May," she said. "We're going to be spending a lot of time together, so I don't see the need for formality." She peered at Elizabeth. "I suppose you're Elizabeth?"

Elizabeth nodded. "It's nice to meet you," she said. She wasn't sure she meant it.

May looked back and forth from Jessica to Elizabeth. "How in the world am I going to tell you two apart? I think I'll have you wear nametags."

Steven started to laugh.

"What's so funny?" May asked him. "I don't enjoy being laughed at."

"Oh, um, nothing," Steven said.

"I'm *not* wearing a nametag," Jessica said. "You can tell us apart by our hair. I wear mine down, and Elizabeth wears hers up." She went over to the counter and took a cookie out of the jar.

"Hold it right there, young lady," May said.

Jessica looked over her shoulder. "What?"

"You can't eat any cookies before dinner," May said. "It's bad nutrition."

"My mother always lets me have a cookie when I get home from school," Jessica argued.

"Well, that may be, but while I am in charge, there will be no snacks between meals. If you must have something, drink a glass of juice. It's much better for you." May smoothed her gray hair with her hand. It was tied back in a tight bun. She wore a straight brown skirt, a white blouse, and sturdy brown shoes that reminded Elizabeth of bowling shoes.

Jessica slammed down the top of the cookie jar and went to the refrigerator to get some juice.

Jessica pulled a sheet of paper off of the refrigerator. "What's this? 'House rules, to be followed at all times,' " she read out loud.

"I'd like to have some order around here,"

May said. "While you look them over, I'll pour you all some juice."

Steven and Elizabeth rushed to Jessica's side as she read the rules aloud. " 'Number one, lights out at nine o'clock. There are no exceptions.' "

"We can't go to sleep at nine o'clock!" Steven cried.

"Early to bed, early to rise," May said as she got the juice out of the refrigerator. "It worked for Ben Franklin, and it'll work for you."

"But the good TV shows don't even start until nine," Steven complained.

"See rule number two," May advised, calmly pouring the juice.

" 'Only one hour of TV a day'!" Jessica shouted. "That's not fair!"

"What about the weekend?" Elizabeth asked.

"The rules are the same," May said.

Elizabeth couldn't believe it. She didn't mind the no-TV rule during the week; she was usually too busy to watch much anyway. But the weekend? "Do we have to go to bed at nine on the weekend, too?" she asked.

May nodded.

They read the rest of the list in silence. The remaining rules weren't as ridiculous—they were about keeping stereos down and not running in the house. They were used to rules like that from their parents. But no snacking? Who was May to tell them what they could and couldn't eat? And how were they ever going to go to bed at nine o'clock? What happened to having pizzas delivered for dinner and going to bed whenever they wanted?

"Here's your juice," May said, putting three small glasses on the table.

Jessica frowned at May and drank her juice. She handed May the glass. "Can I have some more?"

May shook her head. "That's it. We'll be eating in a few hours. I don't want to spoil your appetite." She put the glass in the sink.

"I'm still thirsty," Jessica complained.

"Have a glass of water. It's good for you. Everyone should drink at least six glasses of water a day."

"Yeah, if they want to float," Steven said under his breath. Jessica and Elizabeth both laughed.

"All right, I've had just about enough out of you kids." May stood back and scrutinized each one of them. "First you complain about my rules," she said, pointing to Elizabeth. "Then you don't even thank me for getting your juice," she told Jessica. "And I don't appreciate your smart-aleck remarks, young man."

"So sue me," Steven mumbled.

"I won't be treated disrespectfully," May

said, raising her voice. "You children have no manners, and it's time you learned some."

"We're going to learn manners from you?" Jessica asked.

"All right, that's it! You, go straight to your room, and stay there until dinnertime," May ordered Jessica.

"Fine!" Jessica answered.

Elizabeth and Steven watched Jessica stomp up the stairs. "Um, we have to go work on the garage," Elizabeth told May. "I'm sure my parents told you about the sale we're having."

May nodded. "You may work on the garage. Just make sure you don't track any dirt into the house when you're done."

"OK," Steven said. "But, uh, first we have to check with Jessica about something. Come on." He grabbed Elizabeth's arm, and they ran upstairs.

Steven knocked once on Jessica's door. Then he and Elizabeth went in and closed the door behind them. "Whoa!" Steven said. "I feel like I just climbed out of a lion's cage."

"Can you believe her?" Jessica said. "It's like a witch took over our house while we were at school."

"Shhh," Elizabeth said. "If she hears us talking about her, she's going to get even worse."

"Yeah," Steven said softly, "if there's one

thing we don't want, it's more rules. She'll probably say the three of us can't be in a room together at the same time."

Jessica threw up her hands. "Those rules are unbelievable! Why did Mom and Dad pick this woman for us? Do you think they're mad at us about something?"

Elizabeth shook her head. "I'm sure they didn't know she was like this. When they met her, she was probably nice. She just forgot to tell them that she hates kids!"

"You know, she reminds me of Mrs. Schmid, my math teacher," Steven said. "Her nickname is the Dragon Lady."

"May was probably a sergeant in the army or something," Elizabeth commented. "And she keeps forgetting she's not in the army anymore."

"So what do we do now?" Jessica asked.

"I don't know. This is like a bad movie," Steven said. "The Baby-Sitter From Another Planet!"

"I wish she'd go back to whatever planet she came from," Jessica said.

Steven smiled. "Hmm. That's not a bad idea."

"What do you mean?" Elizabeth asked.

"Well, if she's as unhappy taking care of us as we are having her here, maybe she'll decide it's not worth it," Steven said.

"Are you saying we should try to get rid of her?" Elizabeth asked.

"If we do, then it's full speed ahead for our party," Steven said. "And, we won't have to put up with all her dumb rules!"

Four

◇

Elizabeth was in the middle of writing a *Sixers* article when she heard a shrill whistle.

"Dinner is served!" May yelled from downstairs.

"I feel like I just joined the army," she said to Jessica as they walked downstairs.

"Yeah, only we didn't join, we were *drafted*," Steven said. "She'll probably make us do push-ups before we can eat."

Jessica giggled. "We'll get her back, don't worry."

May was standing at the table in the dining room, waiting for them. "Don't forget to wash your hands," she said. "I don't want any germs at the table."

Steven, Jessica, and Elizabeth crowded around the kitchen sink. "Talk about a germ," Steven whispered. They dried their hands and went into the dining room.

"Steven, you sit here," May said, pointing to the chair at the end of the table. "I want Jessica and Elizabeth on either side of the table."

Steven sat down. "Whatever," he said.

Elizabeth took her seat. She looked at the steaming dishes of food on the table and wrinkled her nose. It looked like one of them was spinach and the other was something involving broccoli.

May started to heap large servings of food onto a plate.

"I don't want any spinach," Jessica said. "What's that other junk?"

"That other junk, as you call it, is broccoli casserole," May said. She put a large serving of spinach on the plate and handed it to Jessica. "Spinach is very good for you. Try it—you'll like it."

"I already know I don't like it," Jessica said. She poked at the broccoli casserole. "Yuck."

"Elizabeth, that's not very polite," May said, frowning.

"I hate broccoli!" Jessica said, without bothering to correct May.

May just filled another plate with food and put it in front of Elizabeth. "Jessica, I don't want to hear anything out of you, either. This is very healthy food."

Elizabeth noticed that Jessica had put her hair in a ponytail and changed into a blue oxford shirt like the one she was wearing. This was certainly one way to annoy May. "I'm Elizabeth. Is this chicken?" She pointed to the third clump of food.

May nodded. "It's chicken cacciatore."

Elizabeth heaved a sigh of relief. At least that was one thing she could eat! She liked some vegetables, but broccoli and spinach didn't happen to be among them.

"Can I make a salad instead?" Jessica asked.

"That's *may* I make a salad," May said. "And no, you may not. I've made you perfectly good food."

"But I'll get sick," Jessica complained.

"Elizabeth, one more word out of you, and you can wash all of the dishes tonight," May said.

Elizabeth could see that Jessica was having a great time making May think she was Elizabeth. It *was* pretty funny, but she didn't feel like cleaning a crusty broccoli casserole dish. That really would make her sick.

Steven didn't say anything about the food. He ate the chicken, but the second he tasted the spinach, he made a face. "Isn't something burning in the kitchen?" he asked.

May sniffed the air. "I don't think so."

"Maybe you left the oven on," Steven said.

"Perhaps I did." May got up and walked into the kitchen.

The second she was gone, Steven ran over to the window, opened it, and flung his food off the plate into the yard. Jessica and Elizabeth jumped up to do the same thing, but May came back into the room just as they made it to the window. Steven was already back in his seat, licking his fork clean.

"What are you doing?" May asked.

"Oh, uh, we thought we saw, uh, a rabbit out there," Elizabeth said.

"Get back into your seats and finish your dinner," May told them. "You shouldn't run around in the middle of a meal!"

Elizabeth looked at Steven's empty plate and sighed. Why hadn't she thought of that? She picked up her fork and tried to work her way through the spinach. She felt like she was eating seaweed.

"Elizabeth, stop mashing your food—it's bad manners," May said.

Elizabeth looked up, but May was talking to Jessica. "Can I be excused?" Jessica whined.

"No, you *may* not be excused," May said. "I want you to clean your plate. Look, Steven's already finished." She smiled at him.

Steven smiled back.

"We're having tapioca pudding for dessert,

and then after that, I thought we'd go for a walk," May said. She put a second helping of spinach on her plate.

"A walk?" Steven said.

"You should always stretch your legs after a big meal," May said. "I go for a two-mile walk every evening."

"Two miles?" Jessica looked at May as if she had lost her mind.

"That's nothing," May said. "When I was a little girl, I had to walk twice that far just to get to school every day."

"So," Jessica said. "That doesn't mean we have to. I have a lot of stuff to do tonight."

"Elizabeth, right now I want you to finish your broccoli," May said.

Jessica sighed and glanced at Elizabeth's plate. They both still had a long way to go.

Steven brushed his hands on his jeans and looked around the garage. He and the twins had been working on it since their after-dinner walk with May. It seemed like the best way of avoiding her. "I think we're finished."

Everything was neatly organized and spread out on tables for Thursday's big sale. There were old dishes, lamps, books, jewelry, and appliances. They had hung used clothes on a clothesline down the middle of the garage to separate the things that were for sale from those that weren't. Mrs. Wakefield had set aside some boxes of things that belonged to her family in one corner of the garage and told the twins to be careful not to let anyone touch her antiques, because they were very valuable and had once belonged to her ancestors.

"I hope we make some money from this," Elizabeth said. She threw an old blanket over the boxes of antiques, to make sure no one touched them. "Do you think people will come tomorrow?"

"We put up ads all over town," Jessica said. "And everyone at school knows about it. I'm sure we'll make some money."

Steven grinned at Jessica. "At least enough for our party supplies."

"So you want to go ahead with Operation Out-the-Door?" Jessica asked.

Steven nodded. "Definitely. Elizabeth?"

"I guess so," Elizabeth replied. Normally she didn't believe in being mean to people, but after what happened that night at dinner, she felt that May deserved a dose of her own medicine. Every once in a while she remembered what she'd eaten for dinner, and her stomach turned. Even cafeteria food was better than May's.

"When do we start?" Elizabeth asked.

Steven put his arm around her shoulder. "That's the spirit!"

"You can leave the first part of the plan to me," Jessica said. "In fact, I've already put one of my ideas into action."

They had just come in from the garage when they heard a loud shriek from upstairs. "What's going on?" Elizabeth asked.

May came running down the stairs. She pointed at her head with a brush. "Who did this?"

"Did what?" Steven answered.

May took the towel off her head. "This!" she cried, holding up her wet hair.

"Your hair is purple!" Elizabeth exclaimed.

May frowned at her. "I know that. I want to know which one of you is responsible!"

"Responsible?" Jessica repeated.

"Well, I certainly didn't *decide* to dye my hair purple," May said angrily. "Steven, I want an apology."

"I didn't do anything," Steven said truthfully.

May raised one eyebrow and looked at Jessica. "Then it was you, Elizabeth."

"I'm Jessica," she replied coolly, "and I didn't do anything, either."

"I didn't either," Elizabeth said. "Maybe there's something wrong with your shampoo."

"There wasn't anything wrong with it yesterday," May grumbled. "Well! I'll deal with you later." She headed back up the stairs to Mr. and Mrs. Wakefield's bedroom, where she was staying.

When she was gone, Jessica started giggling. "With that hair she looks even more like a witch!"

"What did you do?" Elizabeth asked.

"I put the dye we used last Halloween into her shampoo bottle while she was washing the dishes," Jessica explained.

"Nice move," Steven said, nodding with approval.

Jessica smiled. "You haven't seen anything yet."

At that moment, May came charging back down the stairs, still wearing her robe and slippers. "All right, what have you done with my clothes?" She looked from Elizabeth to Jessica to Elizabeth, trying to tell them apart.

"I don't know what you're talking about," Steven said.

"I left them on the bed, and now they're nowhere to be found," May said.

"Maybe you put them back in your suitcase," Jessica suggested.

"No, I didn't." May tapped her foot against the floor. "I'm going to find my clothes, and when

I do, you'll have a lot of explaining to do." They followed her up to Jessica's room where she started hunting through the piles on Jessica's floor. "This room is a mess," she said. "We'll have to take care of that immediately."

"Uh-oh, your plan might be backfiring," Elizabeth whispered.

While May hunted through the bedrooms, Jessica ran downstairs. She came back up with May's clothes and returned them to her bed. When May came back out into the hallway, Jessica said, "Are you sure you looked everywhere in your bedroom?"

"Yes, I did," May insisted.

Jessica tapped her chin with her finger. "That's strange. I could have sworn I saw something lying on the bed that looked exactly like the skirt you were wearing tonight."

May hurried into her bedroom and came out a few seconds later, carrying her clothes.

"Well, look at that," Jessica said.

"That's great—where did you find them?" Steven asked.

"On the bed," May said.

"Isn't that where you left them?" Elizabeth asked.

May shook her head. "Yes, but—"

"Maybe you're overtired," Jessica said. "You

should probably go to bed early tonight. You know, it could be that disease—what's that called? Where old people forget stuff."

"Senility," Steven said, stifling a giggle.

May turned on her heel and marched back into her bedroom. She slammed the door.

Jessica followed Elizabeth into her bedroom and jumped up and down on the bed. "I bet she'll leave tonight. She's probably packing right now."

Elizabeth was just starting to feel a tiny bit sorry for May when a loud whistle sounded outside her door. "Children! Come here immediately!" May yelled.

Jessica rolled her eyes. "Oh, great. It's Sergeant Brown."

She and Elizabeth opened the door just as May blew the whistle again, and it was so loud, they jumped back into the room.

"Come on, you two," May said. Steven was looking down the hall at May suspiciously. "You too, Steven." She pointed to a spot on the floor. "Line up right here."

Steven, Elizabeth, and Jessica took a few steps toward the spot, but that was all.

"We seem to have gotten off to a bad start with one another," May began. "I'm not sure why. I don't usually have this much trouble. But it's been a long time since I was responsible for three children your age." She paused, then said, "I do have several rules, and maybe you don't agree with all of them. That doesn't give you the right to interfere with my private things. Now, who would like to apologize first?"

No one said anything. Steven shifted from his left foot to his right foot.

"I think one of you needs to apologize," May said. "I'm not going anywhere until you do."

"Fine," Jessica replied. She turned and walked down the hall to her room.

"Come back here this instant, Elizabeth!" May called.

Jessica kept walking.

"I said, stop!"

Jessica turned around. "Oh, I didn't know you were talking to me. I'm not Elizabeth."

"And stop trying to confuse me! Now get back here, young lady. Didn't I tell you not to move?"

"You said you weren't going anywhere," Jessica replied. "You didn't say we couldn't."

"That's it!" May cried. "I tried to reason with you, but it's impossible. You children have no manners. It's obvious that your parents don't care if you misbehave."

"That's not true," Elizabeth protested. "And we'd apologize, only—"

May held up her hands. "No, it's too late

for apologies. I'm giving each of you chores as punishment. It'll give you time to think about what you've done. Jessica, clean your room— from top to bottom—and then empty all the wastebaskets in the house. Elizabeth, I want you to clean the bathrooms. Steven, you'll dust the house."

"I'll *what*?" he asked.

"You heard me."

"Now?" Elizabeth asked. "We're supposed to be in bed in an hour. What about our homework?"

"You can finish that in the morning." May adjusted the whistle that hung on a string around her neck.

"But we don't have time in the morning," Jessica said. "We have to be at school at eight."

"Nonsense! There's plenty of time when you get up at five-thirty," May said. "It's time you children were on a decent schedule." She blew the whistle and motioned for them to follow her. "Remember, early to bed, early to rise!"

Elizabeth shook Jessica's arm. "Come on, Jess, it's almost time."

"Oh no, is it five-thirty?" Jessica pulled the covers over her head. "Don't make me get up, Elizabeth. Tell her I'm sick."

"No, silly, it's time for May to get up!"

"Right!" Jessica flung off the covers and got

out of bed. She and Elizabeth crept across the hall and put their ears against the door to the master bedroom.

Elizabeth looked at her watch. It was 3:44 in the morning. "Any second now," she said.

Suddenly, there was a loud ringing from inside the room. "Agh!" they heard May cry.

Jessica bit her lip and looked at Elizabeth. "Success number one," she whispered. They listened as May got out of bed and searched for the alarm clock. Earlier that evening Jessica had wedged it down behind the headboard, so May wouldn't be able to find it for a minute or two. Finally, the alarm was shut off, and they heard May crawl back into bed.

Five minutes later, Elizabeth was practically asleep in the hall when she heard loud music blaring from inside May's room. She and Jessica listened to May get out of bed again and run across the room to the clock radio on the bureau. Earlier that evening, while Jessica had distracted May, Elizabeth had set the clock radio for 3:50 A.M.—and she'd tuned it to the station that played the loudest and most obnoxious heavy metal music. She had also removed the on-off switch.

"We'd better get back to bed," Elizabeth said. As they tiptoed back to their rooms, the music went off. Then May's door opened. Elizabeth practically leaped into her bed, being as quiet as she could.

A moment later her door opened and she pretended to be sound asleep. May walked through the bathroom to Jessica's room, and Jessica let out a loud and very convincing snore.

Five

◇

"Rise and shine!" May bellowed Thursday morning.

Jessica groaned and climbed out of bed. She got dressed as quickly as she could. "Elizabeth, are you ready?" she called through the bathroom.

Elizabeth stood in the doorway. "I guess so. I don't think I've ever gotten up this early. It feels weird." She walked over and pulled up the shade in her room. "There's hardly any light outside."

"The only thing that made me get up was thinking about how tired May's going to look," Jessica said as she brushed her hair.

There was a loud whistle in the hallway. "Breakfast's ready!"

"I wonder if we have to eat anything gross," Jessica said as they headed downstairs.

"Like a spinach omelette?" Elizabeth asked, grinning at her sister.

Jessica wrinkled her nose. "Yuck!"

"Good morning, girls," May greeted them. She sounded peppy, but there were dark circles under her eyes. She seemed to be squinting at them through her glasses.

"You know, May, you look really tired," Jessica said. "Do you think that maybe it's too early to be eating breakfast?"

"Nonsense!" May set some glasses of orange juice on the table. "I get up at this time every morning. But as a matter of fact, I didn't sleep very well."

Jessica shrugged and sat down next to Elizabeth. "Well, you know how it is in a strange bed."

"Something very strange happened last night," May continued. "All of the alarm clocks in your parents' bedroom went off at once." She set a jar of orange marmalade on the table right in front of Jessica and peered into her eyes.

"Mom and Dad must have set them before they left," Elizabeth said quickly.

May turned her gaze on Elizabeth. "For three-forty-five in the morning?"

"Sometimes my dad likes to get up and work then," Jessica said. "That way the house is quiet and he can concentrate."

"Hmm." May brought a plate of English muffins to the table. "Your parents didn't strike me as the kind of people who would wake up to extremely *loud* rock music."

"Oh, they're pretty young, you know," Jessica said. "They're always listening to stuff like that."

May sat down opposite Elizabeth and studied her for a moment. "And when I tried to turn off the radio, I couldn't find the switch."

Elizabeth laughed nervously. "Oh, that knob's always coming off. Dad's always complaining about it!"

Jessica smiled at Elizabeth. She was proud of her twin. She hardly ever lied—but she was doing a good job. May gave up the questioning and got the cereal out of the cabinet. Jessica was glad that at least they were eating a normal breakfast. Then she had a terrible thought. What if May made them go for a walk after breakfast? What if someone from school saw Jessica following an old lady around the block? That would be humiliating.

Steven came downstairs a few minutes later. "Man, I'm beat," he said.

May smiled at him. "Once you get used to this schedule, you'll never give it up."

When she turned back to the counter, Steven mouthed, "Yeah, right" to the twins. "You know,

I could really go for a cup of coffee," he said to May when she turned back around.

Jessica looked at him suspiciously. He never drank coffee. He'd tried it once and said it tasted terrible.

"I haven't made any," May said. "I thought you kids were too young for coffee."

"Are you kidding? I have it every morning," Steven said. "I think I'll make a pot. Would you like some?"

May seemed taken aback by his niceness. "Why, certainly. That would be lovely. Don't make it too strong, though—that's not good for you."

"Oh, I never do," Steven said cheerfully. He took a filter out of the cupboard and put it in the coffee machine. Then he put some coffee in. He glanced over his shoulder, and when he saw that May wasn't looking, he took some spices out of the cupboard and added them to the coffee. Then he poured water into the machine, and turned it on to start brewing.

After a minute or so, a spicy smell started to fill the kitchen. "What is that?" May asked.

"Cinnamon," Steven said, buttering an English muffin. "I always add it to coffee. Smells good, doesn't it?"

May sniffed the air. "Yes, I guess so."

Jessica nudged her brother's leg under the

table with her foot. She had a feeling this was going to be good.

Steven stood up and poured the coffee into two mugs. He handed one to May, and then took a big gulp out of the one he held. "Not bad, if I do say so myself." He nodded. "Not too much cinnamon—just enough to make it taste different."

May added some milk to her coffee, then took a sip. She looked puzzled, so she took another sip. Suddenly, her eyes filled with water, and her face turned red. She jumped up from the table and ran down the hall to the bathroom.

Steven clapped his hands together. "All right!"

"Steven, what did you put in there?" Elizabeth asked.

"Cinnamon," Steven replied with a serious face.

"And?" Elizabeth prompted.

"Garlic powder, a couple of bay leaves, some cayenne pepper, and a few dashes of tabasco sauce!" Steven grinned and took a bite of his muffin.

Jessica grinned. "How come you didn't choke?"

"Because I only pretended to drink it," Steven said. "She drank about half the cup!"

Jessica giggled. "Did you see the look on her face?"

Elizabeth glanced down the hall. "I hope she's not sick."

"She'll get over it. She's just going to be brushing her teeth for the next few weeks," Steven said.

"Hey, I have an idea," Jessica said. "Why don't you offer to cook dinner tonight? She'd be gone in no time!"

May returned to the kitchen five minutes later. Her face was still pink, but she looked more determined than ever. "Steven, don't ever try a stunt like that again. It's just as I thought—you were brought up to behave like monsters. I don't know how your parents expect anyone to look after you!"

"Well, we don't really *need* anyone to look after us," Steven said. "That's why we were thinking, you know, anytime you want to go—"

"I'm not going anywhere!" May replied. "Your parents hired me to take care of you. That's what I'm trying to do. Now, go up and finish your homework. There's still an hour before you have to leave for school."

Jessica felt the disappointment set in as she carried her bowl to the sink. If their pranks last night and Steven's trick this morning hadn't convinced May to leave, nothing would. They just had to think of something else. There was no way she was canceling her party.

"Oh, and another thing," May said. "Until all of these shenanigans come to an end, I've decided to take away your phone privileges."

Jessica spun around. "What?"

"Until you can learn to behave, you're not allowed to use the phone," May said, wiping off the table with a sponge. She didn't look at them when she spoke.

"You can't do that!" Steven argued.

"We have to use the phone sometimes," Elizabeth said.

Jessica couldn't even argue. She was in shock. How was she supposed to exist without a phone? And what if her friends called her, and May told them she wasn't allowed to use the phone? What a way for them to find out she'd lied about not having a baby-sitter. Not only did they have a baby-sitter, they had a tyrant.

"I'm sorry, but until you prove to me that you can behave, the only person in this house who can use the phone is me," May said.

"I bet you don't even have any friends to call!" Jessica said angrily. Then she stomped upstairs, with Elizabeth close on her heels.

"Can you believe her?" Jessica cried after she slammed her bedroom door behind her. "We have to get up at the crack of dawn. *Before* the crack of dawn. We can't watch TV. We had to clean the whole house. And now she won't let us use the phone! You know what, Elizabeth? She's gone too far. This means war!"

Six

◇

Elizabeth rushed home right after school on Thursday afternoon. The garage sale was supposed to start at three o'clock, and she wanted to be ready when it did.

May was waiting in the kitchen when Elizabeth walked in. "Hello," she said, "how was school?"

"Fine," Elizabeth said. "Is Steven home?"

"Not yet. Where's Elizabeth?" May asked.

"I *am* Elizabeth."

May frowned. "Honestly, I don't know why you have to look so much alike."

"We can't help it," Elizabeth told her.

"Well, where's Jessica then?" May asked.

"She had to stay after for a meeting," Elizabeth said. "She'll be here soon."

"Are you ready for the sale?" May asked.

Elizabeth put her knapsack down on the floor. "I think so."

"Are you sure?" May asked. "You know, having a garage sale isn't easy. There's a lot to keep track of."

We can handle it," Elizabeth said firmly. "It's not like we're little kids."

"Hmm. I'm not so sure about that," May said. "We're running out of some essentials. I'm going to go out and do some grocery shopping."

"I thought my parents stocked the kitchen before they left," Elizabeth said.

"Yes, but we're low on fruit juice and vegetables." May took a piece of paper off the counter and skimmed it. "I want to pick up some more milk, too."

Elizabeth shrugged. She could just picture May coming home with a bag full of spinach, Brussels sprouts, and lima beans.

"Keep an eye on your cash box," May said, stopping at the front door as she put on her jacket. "And make sure no one walks on the flowerbed."

"OK," Elizabeth said with a sigh. If May stayed another minute, she was going to go crazy!

"And don't do anything rash while I'm gone," May said on her way out the door.

"I won't!" Elizabeth cried.

May stepped back into the kitchen. "Elizabeth, don't take that tone with me. I've had just about enough of your attitude."

Elizabeth didn't respond. She was sick of May's attitude, too.

"When your parents call, I don't want to have to tell them that you've been a problem," May continued. "Now, can I leave you here all by yourself?"

"Yes," Elizabeth replied, trying to stay calm.

"I'll be back soon," May said, finally closing the door behind her.

"Don't hurry!" Elizabeth yelled at the door. As soon as she heard the car pull out of the driveway, she ran to the cookie jar. She had been dying for a cookie all afternoon. But when she opened the jar, she discovered it was empty. Either Steven had raided it during the night, or—she pulled out a note from the bottom of the jar. "No cookies between meals," it said. Elizabeth slammed the top back on in frustration. This was too much!

Elizabeth went out to the garage and made the final preparations for the sale. She put a new, bigger sign out on their lawn. Then she opened the garage door, sat down at the table they'd set up the night before, and waited for customers to arrive.

After about fifteen minutes, a few cars had pulled up and people had begun looking through the garage. She sold an old game for $3, a jacket for $2, and a toaster for $2.50 to a woman who collected old toasters. "I don't even care if it works," she told Elizabeth. "I have a whole shelf full of toasters!"

Elizabeth thought she was a little odd, but she just smiled and gave the woman her change.

She was showing a girl their collection of old hats when she felt someone tug at her sleeve. She turned around and saw Amy standing next to a tall boy with blond hair. "Hi, Elizabeth! How's the sale going?" she asked.

"OK, I guess," Elizabeth said. "Just a second." She finished showing the different hats to the girl, who looked like she was about sixteen.

"I'll take this one," the girl said, holding up a floppy blue velveteen hat. "It's so ugly, it's cool!"

Elizabeth laughed. "That's two dollars," she said.

"Two?" The girl searched her jean pockets and came up with a dollar. "I have only one. Any chance you'd make a deal?"

"Well . . ." Elizabeth looked at the hat. She couldn't think of anyone else who would want to buy it. "OK."

"Thanks! Thanks a lot!" The girl put the hat on over her long black curly hair and practically skipped down the driveway.

"What a weirdo," the boy with Amy commented.

"Elizabeth, this is Rob," Amy said. She put her arm through his. "Rob, this is my best friend, Elizabeth."

"Are you hard up for money or something?" Rob asked, glancing around the garage. Amy giggled.

"No," Elizabeth said, a little put off by Rob's comment. "We're trying to raise some money for charity, and some for ourselves, too."

"That girl was a charity!" Rob said with a laugh. "Did you see her outfit? She probably won the Worst Dressed category in her yearbook." Amy laughed again.

"I like it when people dress differently," Elizabeth said, defending the girl. "I mean, she has her own style."

"That's for sure," Rob scoffed.

"So, have you made a lot of money so far?" Amy asked.

"Not really," Elizabeth said.

"Hey, are you going to play any good music at your party Saturday?" Rob asked. "Or should I bring some of my tapes?"

"That depends. What music do you like?" Elizabeth asked.

"Everything except the Emerald Girls, or whatever they're called," Rob said, naming one of Amy's favorite groups.

Amy giggled. "Oh, I hate them, too."

Elizabeth couldn't believe it! Amy was acting totally unlike herself. And why did she giggle after everything Rob said? He wasn't funny—he was mean!

"I really like Johnny Gordon and the Waves," Rob continued. "Why don't you try to hire them for your party?"

Elizabeth practically burst out laughing. That was one of the worst bands she had ever heard! She and Amy had spent a whole night imitating them once. "Um, I don't think so," Elizabeth said. "Sorry."

"Let's go," Rob said. "I think I have all the old hair driers I need. If we stay here too long, we might actually buy something."

"Well, OK," Amy said. She cast an apologetic glance at Elizabeth. "We're going over to Rob's to try out a new video game he got for his birthday."

"Prepare to lose," Rob said as he walked down the driveway.

"See you later, Amy!" Elizabeth called after her friend. She wanted to like Rob for Amy's sake, but Elizabeth hoped Amy wouldn't go out with him for long. She didn't know if she could take it.

"How much do we have so far?" Jessica asked.

Elizabeth counted the money in the box.

"Thirteen dollars and twenty-five cents. And a coupon for free games the next time we go bowling."

"Oh, great." Jessica leaned back and put her feet up on the table. "Maybe it's a good thing we can't have the party. We'd only be able to buy one bag of chips and a bottle of soda."

Steven was busy showing their old board games to a man wearing round glasses. "See, you have to answer these questions, and then you get a chance to swing on this vine. But if you hit a tree, you lose everything," he explained.

The man pushed his glasses up on his nose. "I don't think so," he said. "Thank you, though." He looked at a few other things, then walked down to his car and drove away.

He had only been gone for a few minutes when May's car pulled into the driveway. "I hope she doesn't hang around out here," Steven said. "She'd scare off all the customers."

"All *what* customers?" Jessica said.

May got out of the car and took a bag of groceries from the trunk. "Steven, I could use some help carrying in these bags," she said.

Steven sighed loudly and went off to help May.

"I'm thirsty," Elizabeth said. "I think I'll go get some lemonade. Do you want some?"

"Sure, if she'll let you have any," Jessica said.

"I'll be right back."

Jessica sighed and looked up and down the street. No one was headed for the Wakefields' garage sale. Not that it even mattered. With May around, it was going to be impossible to have their party.

At the Unicorn meeting that afternoon, everyone had given Jessica all kinds of suggestions for her party. Janet had said that a lot of eighth graders she knew planned on coming. Jessica just couldn't tell them the party wasn't going to happen. There had to be a way to convince May to leave before Saturday . . . but how?

A big, old car pulled up in front of the house and a man walked up to the garage. "How's it going?" he asked, smiling at Jessica. He was wearing a baseball cap, a striped sweater, and old, faded jeans. His high-top sneakers were scuffed and dirty.

"All right," she said.

"Wow, you have a lot of things in there," he commented. "OK if I look around?"

"Sure," Jessica replied. "Everything's for sale."

"Fine. I'll just take a look then."

Jessica watched as he poked around in the garage for a minute or so. He spent a long time examining her parents' ancient record albums. Looking at the albums only reminded Jessica of all the compact discs Lila had promised to bring to the party.

Jessica leaned forward and put her elbows on the table. She rested her chin in her hands and tried to think of a plan.

All they needed to do was get May out of the house for a few hours . . . All of a sudden, she realized she had been staring right at the answer to her problems—May's car! If they could get her to go somewhere in her car, and then get lost, or run out of gas, or both—there'd be no way she could make it home in time to stop the party!

"Excuse me?" the man who had been browsing in the garage asked.

Jessica jumped. She had forgotten there was anybody in there beside her.

The man held up a small glass case which contained a carved wooden rose. "How much is this?"

Jessica didn't recognize it right away. She couldn't remember seeing it on one of the tables, but there was so much stuff, she wasn't surprised.

"I'll give you fifty dollars for it," the man said cheerfully.

Jessica practically fell off her chair. Fifty dollars? They could stop the sale right there and get to work on her plan. Still, she didn't want to overcharge him too much. Most of the stuff was under ten dollars.

"OK, seventy-five then," The man held out some bills. "And I'll give you cash, too. Is it a deal?"

"Sure," Jessica said. "You really like it, huh?"

"It's a treasure," the man said, examining the rose.

Jessica handed him five dollars in change. "Thank you very much," she said.

"No, thank you!" he said.

Jessica counted and recounted the four twenty-dollar bills in her hand. Eighty dollars! This was better than she had possibly imagined. When they added that to what they already had, and split it in two, they'd have almost fifty dollars.

The door to the kitchen opened and Elizabeth walked out, carrying a glass. "She made me wait until she squeezed the lemons herself," Elizabeth explained. "She said it's healthier that way."

"Elizabeth, look at this!" Jessica waved the money in front of her sister's face. "You are not going to believe what just happened. This guy came and spent seventy-five dollars on a little wooden rose. Seventy-five dollars! Can you believe it?"

"Jessica, we didn't have anything like that for sale," Elizabeth said, looking concerned. "That one sounds familiar, though." She walked around the garage and stopped all of a sudden. "Oh, no!"

"What?" Jessica asked.

Elizabeth pointed to the boxes of antiques in the back of the garage. The blanket that had been covering them was thrown to one side, and they were all open. Elizabeth searched through them quickly. "Jessica, you just sold our great-great-great-grandmother's rose!" she cried. "That's one of Mom's favorite things in the whole wide world!"

Seven

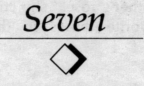

"Where were you guys?" Steven asked. He was sitting at the table in front of the garage with his feet propped on its edge.

Elizabeth had to stop to catch her breath for a moment before she answered. "We were chasing a car."

Steven looked at her like she was crazy. "Why? I mean, I know things around here are pretty boring, but—"

"It was an emergency," Elizabeth said.

"I know—some guy you like went by in a car, and you two were chasing him, right?" Steven asked.

"Ha ha," Jessica said. "Very funny."

"Jessica sold one of the antiques," Elizabeth said. "Remember that carved wooden rose that belonged to Mom's great-great-grandmother?"

"No," Steven said.

"It was in one of those boxes that were off limits," Elizabeth said glumly.

"Uh-oh," Steven said. "Mom and Dad are going to kill us. Those things are worth a lot of money."

"I know," Elizabeth said. "It's not just that, either. That was the only thing Mom had that belonged to her great-great-grandmother. She told me about it when we were sorting through the things after you guys went inside on Monday night. It means a lot to her." It was going to break her mother's heart when she discovered the rose was gone. Mrs. Wakefield had told Elizabeth all about her great-great-grandmother. Her name was Alice Larson, and she had come to the United States from Sweden when she was sixteen. Elizabeth's mother had been named after her.

"So how come she didn't have it in the house if it meant so much to her?" Jessica asked.

Elizabeth frowned at her. "She said it was really fragile, and she didn't want to break it," Elizabeth explained. "Jessica, how could you have done that?"

Jessica took a sip of lemonade. "I don't know, I guess I didn't notice what it was."

"How could you not notice?" Elizabeth asked.

"I was thinking about something important, and all of the sudden this man offered me seventy-five dollars for it, so of course I said yes," Jessica told her. "I don't know. I thought he was a little weird, but he wanted to pay that much. I guess I didn't really think about it."

"You can say that again," Elizabeth said.

"Hey, it could have happened to anybody," Steven said. "Don't get all hyper about it."

"But you don't understand," Elizabeth said. "We absolutely have to get that rose back. Don't you get it? Mom and Dad trusted us to do this on our own, and now we messed up and lost something really valuable. Mom's never going to forgive us." What Elizabeth was really thinking was that her mother was never going to forgive *her*. Even though it was really Jessica's fault, Elizabeth was the one Mrs. Wakefield had told all about her great-great-grandmother.

"Hey, the afternoon wasn't a total waste," Jessica announced with a smile. "I thought of a plan to get May out of the house so we can still have our party!"

"Wait a second," Elizabeth said, turning to her twin. "What did that man look like?"

Jessica chewed her thumbnail while she tried to remember. "He had on these old, faded jeans," she began. "And a blue striped sweater. He had on the world's oldest pair of sneakers, too."

"What color hair did he have?" Elizabeth asked.

"Brown, I think," Jessica said. "Yeah, brown and curly. But he had on a baseball cap over it. I didn't pay that much attention to him, because he looked like he couldn't afford anything," she said. "You saw his car—it was a boat!"

"Did you get the license plate number?" Steven teased.

"I wish we did," Elizabeth said seriously. "Then maybe I could track him down. I don't know how I'm going to find him, but I'm going to try." She headed for the house.

"Wait, Elizabeth! Don't you want to hear my great plan?" Jessica called after her. "The bash of the year is back on!"

Elizabeth shook her head. "Go ahead, do whatever you want," she replied. "I have something more important to take care of." *And it's all your fault, Jessica!* she felt like adding.

Elizabeth went into the house and started flipping through the phone book for the names of antique dealers. She figured the man might try to resell the rose, since it was probably worth a lot more than seventy-five dollars. It was worth a lot more than that to her mother, Elizabeth knew.

Remembering May's rule about not using the phone, Elizabeth decided to look around the house and see if May would notice. She wasn't downstairs, so Elizabeth tiptoed upstairs and peeked into the master bedroom. May was stretched out on the bed with a quilt over her, taking a nap.

Elizabeth tiptoed back downstairs and quickly picked up the phone. She wanted to call as many antique dealers as she could. She had a mystery to solve—and it wasn't going to be easy!

"So what do you think?" Jessica asked Steven when she had finished describing her plan for Saturday night.

"It sounds good," Steven said. "Do you think it'll work?"

"It worked on 'Days of Turmoil,'" Jessica said. She sipped her lemonade. "She'll fall for it."

"We'll have to make sure everyone leaves by, like, midnight," Steven said.

"No problem."

"I don't know if it'll work, but I'll try anything," Steven said. "There's no way I'm calling off our party because of a cranky old baby-sitter." He looked up and down the street. "Do you think we should bother with this garage sale any longer?"

Jessica shrugged. "Why not? Whatever else we make, we can use for the party."

"Don't forget, we're giving half of the proceeds away," Steven said.

"I know, but we still have almost fifty dollars," Jessica replied. "Let's make a shopping list while we sit here." She took a pen out of their cash box. "OK, what should we get?"

"I know what we shouldn't get," Steven said, making a face. "Fruit juice and vegetables! You should have seen the bags I carried in. She probably bought every pea in the whole store."

"Gee, I wonder what we're having for dinner," Jessica said.

"Well, we have to eat it, and we have to pretend to like it," Steven said.

Jessica let out a loud sigh. "This plan is going to be harder than I thought!"

"May, could you please pass the peas?" Steven asked.

Elizabeth was drinking a glass of water, and she practically choked. She had never heard Steven be so polite—except for that morning, when he'd served May the extra-hot coffee.

May handed the bowl to Steven. "Here you are."

Steven ate a large serving of peas in about two minutes. "Those were great! I've never had such good peas." He dabbed his mouth with a napkin.

"Thank you," May said. "Would you like some more?"

"Uh . . . no thank you," he said. "Could I please have the rolls, though?" He smiled at May.

"Certainly!" May passed the basket of rolls to him, and he took two.

Jessica pointed to the plate in the center of the table. "What do you call this dish?"

"Those are baked stuffed peppers," May replied. "Do you like them?"

"Oh, I love them," Jessica said. "My mom never makes these. Do you think you could leave her the recipe?"

"Of course," May said. She looked around the table at everyone. "You all seem to be in a good mood tonight. I take it your garage sale was a success?"

"It went very well," Jessica said, nodding. "Thank you for asking."

Elizabeth didn't know if her sister had sat out in the sun too long that afternoon or what, but she knew that something was up.

"Elizabeth, you're not eating very much," May observed. "Is everything all right?"

"Yes," Elizabeth said. "I'm just not very hungry, that's all."

"You didn't have any snacks while I was gone, did you?" May asked.

"No," Elizabeth replied truthfully.

"Are you sure?" May asked, looking at her suspiciously.

"Yes, I'm sure," Elizabeth said, exasperated.

"Well, we'll just wait here until you get hungry," May said.

"Great," Elizabeth said.

"Young lady, don't take that tone with me," May said.

"What tone?" asked Elizabeth.

"The same one you used last night," May said, "when you criticized my broccoli casserole."

"That wasn't me, that was Jessica!" Elizabeth protested.

Jessica shot her twin an angry glance across the table.

"Don't blame your sister for something you did," May said. "Now, go ahead and finish your peas."

Elizabeth tried to swallow the peas whole, so she didn't have to taste them. When she was finished, she set her fork down on her plate, making a loud clanking noise.

"Careful," May instructed her. "You might break the china."

Elizabeth turned to Steven and rolled her eyes. She couldn't do anything right.

"I'll wash the dishes," Jessica offered, practically leaping out of her chair.

"And I'll help!" Steven smiled at Jessica.

"That would be very nice," May said. "Thank you."

What's with these two? Elizabeth thought. Either her brother and sister had lost their minds, Elizabeth decided, or they were working on part one of their plan.

"After you're done, we can go for our nightly constitutional," May said cheerfully while she wiped off the table.

"Our what?" asked Jessica.

"Our walk," May told her. "My, they certainly don't teach vocabulary as well as they used to when I was in school."

"Back in the Ice Age," Steven whispered to Jessica as he joined her at the sink, and Elizabeth saw their backs shake with laughter. She was glad they hadn't changed *too* much.

Eight

◇

"Hi, Aaron!" Jessica said, hurrying to catch up with him as he walked down the hall on Friday. "You're still coming tomorrow night, right?"

"To your party, you mean?" Aaron asked. "Sure. Ken and I are going together."

"Great!" Jessica said. "Practically everyone's going to be there."

Aaron smiled at Jessica and ran a hand through his brown hair. "Uh, should I bring anything?"

"Nope!" Jessica said cheerfully. "All you have to do is show up."

"OK, well, I'll see you later," Aaron said. "Bye."

"Bye, Aaron." Jessica smiled. She was so happy that she had to restrain herself from leaping up into the air.

"What are you so happy about?"

Jessica turned and saw Lila standing beside her. "I just talked to Aaron."

"Oh," Lila said. "Is he still coming to your party?"

Jessica nodded. "He said he couldn't wait." That wasn't exactly what he said, but she knew that was what he meant.

"How was your garage sale yesterday?" Lila asked.

"Fine," Jessica said. "We made a lot of money. I thought you were going to come."

"I was, only when I got home it was so hot I decided to go swimming instead," Lila said. "Sorry."

"I know it was hot. I had to sit out in the sun all afternoon," Jessica said. "But it was worth it. Now we're all ready for the party."

"How many people are coming?" Lila asked.

"Lots," Jessica said. "You're going to come early with your CDs, right?"

Lila nodded. "I'll be there at seven. My dad's going to drop me off on his way to dinner."

"You didn't tell your father that we're having a party, did you?" Jessica was worried that parents might call and want to talk to her parents.

"No, silly," Lila said. "No one's *that* dumb. The only thing you have to worry about is Caroline Pearce." Caroline was the biggest gossip at

Sweet Valley Middle School, and she lived two doors down from the Wakefields.

"I had to invite her, just so she won't talk," Jessica admitted. "But don't worry, she won't ruin the party."

"No, she'll probably write about it in her next *Sixers* column, though," Lila said. Caroline was also the gossip columnist for the newspaper.

"We'll get Elizabeth to take it out," Jessica said. "If any parents see that paper, we'll all be in trouble. Anyway, it will be fine. We're going to have a great time! Especially me and Aaron."

Friday at noon, Elizabeth ran into Brooke Dennis in the lunch line. "Hi, Brooke, how are you?" she said.

Brooke shrugged. "OK, I guess. Jessica told me you guys are having a party this weekend."

"Yeah, I guess so," Elizabeth said. "Can you come?"

"I'm not sure yet," Brooke said. "My mother wrote and said she's coming for a visit soon. I don't know when. It might be this weekend."

"Wow, that's pretty exciting," Elizabeth said. Brooke's parents were divorced, and she lived with her father. Her mother had moved to Paris, so Brooke didn't get to see her very often.

Brooke nodded and took a bowl of chocolate pudding.

"Do you want to come and sit with me and Amy?" Elizabeth asked.

"I can't today—Olivia and I have to talk about our science project. It's due in a week, and we haven't even started it yet."

"Well, good luck—tell her I said hi," Elizabeth said. She walked over to the table where Amy was saving a seat for her. "Hi, Amy." She sat down and stared at the food on her tray. She wasn't even hungry.

"Elizabeth, is something wrong?" Amy asked.

Elizabeth shrugged. "I'm just not hungry."

"Do you miss your parents?"

"Yes," Elizabeth admitted. "But that's not what's bothering me."

"What is it?" Amy asked. She leaned forward and took a sip of apple juice.

"It's kind of hard to explain. But yesterday we sold something that we weren't supposed to sell. Actually, Jessica was the one who sold it, but I don't think she's going to be a big help in getting it back. I have to figure out how to find it before my parents get home."

"Wow," Amy said. "That's too bad. I'm sure you'll find it, though. Are we still on for ice cream at Casey's? I told Rob we'd meet him there at four."

"I don't know. I'd kind of like to spend the

afternoon looking at antique shops to see if it turns up anywhere," Elizabeth explained.

"If you do that right after school, you'll have at least an hour before you have to meet us," Amy said. "You'll probably be tired of looking by then. And Rob really wants to meet Todd."

"He does?" Elizabeth was surprised.

Amy nodded. "Come on, Elizabeth, please say you'll come. It won't be any fun without you. Finally we *both* have a boyfriend. You can't cancel our first official double date ever. I mean, it's practically an historical event!"

Elizabeth laughed. Amy could always cheer her up, no matter how down she felt. "Well, OK, I guess." She had left May a note saying she had to stay after school late, so that she'd have plenty of time to look for the antique rose.

Amy took a bite of her grilled cheese sandwich. "Are you getting psyched for your party?"

"Well, kind of," Elizabeth said. Despite all of Steven and Jessica's scheming, she still wasn't sure whether they were actually going to pull it off. She would have liked to tell Amy what was really going on, but she and Steven and Jessica had agreed to keep May a secret.

"You don't sound too excited," Amy said. "I think it's going to be great. Rob's looking forward to it, too. If he gets to know Todd today, then he won't feel so out of place on Saturday night. Todd is coming today, isn't he?"

"What about Todd?"

Both Amy and Elizabeth jumped. "I didn't see you!" Elizabeth said, looking up at Todd. He was with Ken Matthews.

"Were you talking about what an amazing person I am?" Todd asked with a grin. He sat down next to Elizabeth, and Ken sat beside Amy.

"Oh, well, that and about this afternoon," Elizabeth said. "Do you still want to go to Casey's with us?"

"Sure," Todd said. "What time?"

"Four," Amy said.

"Sounds great," Ken said. "I'll meet you guys there at four, too, OK?"

Elizabeth glanced at Amy, who tore off a piece of her napkin and threw it on her tray. "Actually, it's not OK," Amy said uncomfortably.

"Hey, I have money this time, if that's what you're worried about," Ken joked.

"No, it's not that," Amy said. "It's just . . . I'm going with someone else."

"Who?" Ken asked.

"This guy I met at the mall." Amy looked at Ken. "His name is Rob, and he's a fantastic soccer player."

"I bet he's not as good as Aaron," Todd said. Elizabeth could tell that he felt uncomfortable, too.

"Yes, he is," Amy said.

Ken stood up and pushed his chair in, loudly scraping it against the floor. "Have a great time," he said. "See you, Todd." He walked out of the cafeteria without looking back.

"I have to go finish my math homework," Amy suddenly announced. She stood up and walked out of the cafeteria, too.

"What's going on with them?" Todd asked.

"I guess Ken still likes Amy, only now she has this new boyfriend," Elizabeth said. "But you know what? I know Amy still likes Ken, too."

"You met her new boyfriend, right? What's he like?" Todd asked, munching on a potato chip.

"He's, um . . . he's all right, I guess," Elizabeth said. "I'll let you judge for yourself."

Elizabeth walked into Valley Antiques and weaved her way in between old tables and lamps up to the sales desk. A man wearing wire-rimmed glasses and a tweed blazer looked up at her. "May I help you?"

"Yes, I hope so," Elizabeth said.

The man stood up and held out his hand. "Martin Hannaford," he said.

Elizabeth shook his hand. "Elizabeth Wakefield," she said. "I'm looking for a carved wooden rose that my sister sold at a garage sale by mistake. I thought whoever bought it might have resold it to you," Elizabeth explained.

"It's possible," Mr. Hannaford said. "What period is it from?"

"I don't know that," Elizabeth said. "But it belonged to my great-great-great-grandmother, and she came from Sweden. It was in a glass case." She made the shape of it with her hands. "It's about this big."

"It sounds absolutely lovely, but I'm afraid I haven't seen it." The man tapped his chin. "Have you checked with Jameson Antiques?"

Elizabeth sighed. "I've been everywhere else in town. No one's seen it."

"You might try calling some of the stores closer to Los Angeles."

"Thanks, but even if they had it, I couldn't get there," Elizabeth said.

"Couldn't your parents drive you?" he asked.

"No, they're out of town, and I need to find it before they get back," Elizabeth said.

"I see. You do have a problem." He smiled and took a business card out of his jacket pocket. "Here, write down your name and phone number, and I'll call if it turns up here. I'll check with some of my friends in the area, too."

"OK, but don't call before Sunday," Elizabeth said. She didn't want May to find out what had happened. "Our phone isn't working, but it'll be fixed by then."

"It sounds like you're having a bad week!"

"You can say that again. Thanks a lot for your help!" Elizabeth called as she walked to the door.

A few minutes later, Elizabeth parked her bike and chained it to the bicycle rack outside the mall. When she walked into Casey's, Todd, Amy, and Rob were already there.

"Sorry I'm late," Elizabeth said, pulling up a chair beside Todd.

"It's OK, we already ate," Rob said.

Amy hit him playfully on the arm. "We did not!"

"Did you find it?" Todd asked.

Elizabeth shook her head. "No, and I've run out of places to look."

Todd gave her a sympathetic smile. "Maybe it'll turn up at someone else's garage sale."

"That's a great idea," Elizabeth said. "I bet there's a lot of them on Saturdays."

"I can help look if you want," Todd said.

"What are you talking about?" Rob asked.

"Elizabeth has to find an antique that belongs to her mom," Amy said.

"Thrillsville!" Rob said. "Hey, I'm hungry. Let's order."

Amy frowned. "It's really important, Rob."

"So is eating! Hey, Todd, have you ever had the Monster Sundae here?" Rob asked.

"No, I haven't," Todd said. "But I heard they're awesome."

"I'm going to get a butterscotch sundae with chocolate ice cream," Amy said. "What are you going to have, Elizabeth?"

"I don't know. I think I'll just have a dish of strawberry frozen yogurt." Elizabeth didn't want to be too full when she got home—it was hard enough to eat May's cooking when she was hungry.

"I hate yogurt," Rob said. "It's so sour. How can you eat it?"

"I like it," Elizabeth said.

"It's so gross. Doesn't it have bacteria in it or something?" Rob asked.

Elizabeth rolled her eyes. Whatever it was that Amy saw in Rob, she hoped Amy would stop seeing it—and him—soon!

"Don't worry, it'll show up," Todd told Elizabeth as they walked out of Casey's. "Sweet Valley's not that big."

"Yeah, I guess you're right," she replied. "But we only have one more day."

"I'll meet you tomorrow at noon, OK?"

"Let's meet at your house," Elizabeth said.

She didn't want May to know about Todd. She'd probably tell Elizabeth that she couldn't start dating until she was eighteen. She didn't want Todd to know about May either.

"Hey, is your party still on for tomorrow?" Todd called over his shoulder.

"I guess so!" Elizabeth shouted back.

"See you!" Todd waved to her as he rode off.

Elizabeth smiled. *Todd is so nice*, she thought. He understood how she was feeling, and he wanted to help. It made her feel much better.

She turned into the driveway and put her bicycle in the garage. She had just stepped into the kitchen when she heard May yell, "Elizabeth, is that you?"

"Yes!" Elizabeth answered.

May came running downstairs. "Where have you been?"

"I had to stay after school to work on the newspaper. You got my note, right?"

"Yes, I did." May frowned at her. "Are you sure you were at school this whole time?"

Elizabeth nodded.

"Tell me the truth, Elizabeth."

"I am telling you the truth," Elizabeth replied calmly. Normally she hated to lie, but somehow with May it was different.

"You stayed after school and worked on the

newspaper until five-fifteen? You didn't go anywhere else?" May folded her arms across her chest
and stared at Elizabeth.

"Yes!" Elizabeth cried, feeling frustrated.

"I don't believe you," May said. "I don't
know why you don't just tell me where you really
were."

"Fine, don't believe me," Elizabeth muttered.

"You know, this isn't the first time you've
lied to me," May continued. "I don't know what
your parents let you get away with, but I'm not
going to put up with it. You've acted like a spoiled
brat ever since I got here."

"What?" Elizabeth stared at May in disbelief.
"I am not a spoiled brat!"

"You've broken every rule—"

"I have not!" Elizabeth cried.

"And now you've interrupted me again. If
you're going to be that inconsiderate, you can just
go to your room right now," May said sternly.

"Fine, I will!" Elizabeth yelled. She grabbed
her knapsack and ran toward the stairs.

"No running in the house!" May called after
her.

"Leave me alone!" Elizabeth said, dashing up
the stairs. She wanted to get as far away from
May as she could. She felt like she was going to
burst into tears. How could May be so mean to
her?

Elizabeth didn't bother knocking on Jessica's door, she just walked into her room. Jessica and Steven were sitting on the bed, talking.

"I don't know what you guys are planning to do to get rid of May," Elizabeth said angrily. "But whatever it is, count me in!"

Nine

◇

Friday night, long after she was supposed to be asleep, Jessica tiptoed downstairs to the living room. May had already gone to bed, and Jessica couldn't resist the temptation to use the phone. It had been such torture not to be able to call her friends for the past three days.

At the Fowler mansion, one of the maids answered the phone. Jessica kept her voice to a whisper as she asked to speak to Lila.

"Hello?" Lila said a minute later.

"Lila, hi," Jessica said softly.

"I thought your phone was broken," Lila said.

"It was, but, uh, they came and fixed it today," Jessica said. "They said it might be broken again tomorrow, so I figured I might as well call people now." Jessica didn't want Lila calling her on Saturday—May might answer and ruin everything.

"How come you're calling so late?" Lila asked.

Jessica glanced at the clock on the wall. It was ten-fifteen. "I was up late planning my party," she said. "I didn't even notice how late it was!"

"Well, I guess I'd stay up late, too, if my father wasn't here," Lila commented.

"Right!" Jessica said. "Actually, I think I'm going to watch the late-late movie. It's so great being able to stay up as long as I want." She loved making Lila jealous. "Steven and I are going to order a pizza, too," she added. What Lila didn't know, wouldn't hurt her!

"When are your parents coming back?" Lila asked.

"Sunday," Jessica said. "Why?"

"Just wondering. You're going to have a lot of cleaning up to do after the party," Lila said.

"That's the last thing on my mind," Jessica said, stretching out on the couch. "The first thing is—"

"Don't tell me—I know, it's Aaron," Lila said.

Jessica giggled. Just then she heard footsteps upstairs—right above the living room. That was the master bedroom. "Lila, I have to go," she said hurriedly. "The, uh, the pizza's here," Jessica said.

"I thought you said you didn't order it yet."

"I'll see you tomorrow night," Jessica whispered. She stood up and quietly replaced the receiver on the phone. Then she crept toward the stairs.

"Jessica, what are you doing down here?" a voice in the kitchen asked. Jessica spun around. May was standing by the kitchen table.

Jessica searched her brain for an excuse. Had May heard her on the phone? "I, uh, came down to get a glass of water," Jessica said. "You know, since I started drinking those six glasses a day, if I don't have enough, I can't sleep."

May nodded. "I know what you mean. But I thought I heard voices down here."

"Well, I was kind of nervous, since it's so dark, so I was talking to myself," Jessica said. "Anyway, I think I'll go back to bed now." She hoped May wouldn't check the sink for dirty glasses before she made her getaway.

"Sleep well!" May said cheerfully.

Jessica took the stairs two at a time. This baby-sitter thing was no big deal, once you learned how to handle her!

On Saturday afternoon, Elizabeth walked into Jessica's room and collapsed on the bed. "Mom's going to kill us," she mumbled into the pillow.

"I guess you didn't find the rose," Jessica said.

Elizabeth lifted her head. "Todd and I looked everywhere. We went to ten different garage sales, and whenever we passed a house with a big, old car parked in front, we rang the doorbell to see if they were the ones who bought it. People thought we were crazy!"

"Wow, I can't believe it disappeared like that," Jessica said. "I put up those signs, you know. Maybe the guy will see one of them and bring it back."

"I doubt it," Elizabeth said.

Jessica tried to think of something to cheer up her sister. She hated seeing her so upset, especially on the day of their big party. "It doesn't really matter when the rose gets returned, as long as Mom gets it back, right? I mean, maybe Mom and Dad will be able to track it down when they get home. Sure, they'll be mad, but they'll forgive you," she said.

Elizabeth raised one eyebrow and frowned at her.

"I mean, us," Jessica added. "I'll tell Mom the truth—it was my fault." She reached over and ruffled her sister's hair. "Come on, Elizabeth, cheer up. It's not going to do any good if you sit around and mope. You might as well have fun.

After all, this is going to be the best party Sweet Valley's ever seen—and it is going to be at our house," she said. "Aren't you looking forward to getting May out of our hair?"

Elizabeth sat up on the bed. "You're not going to believe this, but just now, before I came up here, she made me sweep the patio. She said it was the least I could do."

"She made me vacuum the whole upstairs!" Jessica said. "Then she told me we're having stuffed peppers again for dinner."

Elizabeth laughed. "That's because you told her you liked them so much!"

"Big mistake," Jessica said. It was nice to see Elizabeth laugh—she had been so upset ever since her big fight with May the night before. "But if things work out, we won't have to eat dinner with her."

"Good, I don't think I can stand another meal with her," Elizabeth said. "I might throw my stuffed pepper at her."

"Me, too." Jessica giggled. "Remember when Steven threw his food out the window? I wonder if she ever saw it out there."

"No, he'd probably be in jail if she had," Elizabeth grumbled.

"Let's not talk about her anymore," Jessica said. "It's too depressing. Let's figure out what we're going to wear tonight!"

Elizabeth shrugged. "OK."

Jessica grabbed her sister's hand and pulled her up from the bed. Then she marched through the bathroom to Elizabeth's room. "How about a miniskirt?" She opened the closet and started sorting through Elizabeth's clothes.

"What are you going to wear?" Elizabeth asked.

"I'm not sure," Jessica said. She pulled out a bright pink blouse with thin white lines on it. "Can I borrow this?"

"Jess, we're supposed to be picking out *my* outfit," Elizabeth protested.

Jessica ducked out of the closet. "Don't you want me to look good, too?"

At four o'clock, Elizabeth and Jessica went downstairs to the living room. May was in the kitchen, reading a magazine. They turned on the television and started watching the sports channel.

"Any second now," Jessica whispered to Elizabeth. "I can't wait!"

A couple of minutes later, the door to the kitchen opened and Steven walked in. Jessica and Elizabeth leaned back on the couch and peered around the corner to get a better view.

"Hi," Steven said. He marched straight over to the refrigerator.

"Steven, your shoes are covered with mud!" May cried. "Please take them off before you go any further."

Steven sighed loudly and leaned over to untie his sneakers. He took them off and tossed them over toward the door.

"Careful! How many times have I told you not to throw things in the house?" May said.

"It's my house," Steven retorted.

May didn't say anything, but she looked angry.

Steven took a package of French fries out of the freezer. He put them on the counter and grabbed a plate from the cupboard.

May cleared her throat. "We'll be eating dinner in a few hours," she said.

"I know." Steven dumped some fries onto the plate.

"Steven, I don't approve of snacking in between meals," May said. "You know that."

"I'm hungry," Steven said. "I was playing football all afternoon."

"How about an apple, then," May suggested.

"I don't want an apple," Steven replied. He stared at her angrily, then slid the plate into the microwave oven and pressed the "on" button.

"Steven, you know the rules," May continued. She got up from the table, walked over to the microwave, and shut it off.

Steven pushed it back on and glared at her. "This is my house. If I want to eat French fries, I can."

"Not when I'm in charge," May said coolly. She unplugged the microwave from the wall. "They're bad for you, and—"

"I don't care!" Steven cried. "And I don't care about your stupid rules, either! I'm so sick of eating what you want us to eat and sleeping when you tell us to sleep and getting up at five o'clock every morning. I've tried really hard to do what you want, but it's never good enough. I can't stand living here anymore!" He threw the bag of French fries on the floor and ran upstairs.

Jessica turned to Elizabeth and smiled. "That was fun!" she whispered, and Elizabeth nodded in agreement. Steven had just said everything they'd been wanting to say since the day May arrived!

May was picking up the French fries from the floor when Steven came back downstairs, carrying a knapsack. He sat down to put his sneakers back on.

"Where are you going?" May demanded.

Steven didn't answer right away. He just tied his sneaker laces.

"Steven, I asked you a question," May said. "Where are you going?"

Steven stood up and hoisted his knapsack

onto his back. "As far away from you as I can get!" he said. "And I'm not coming back, either!" He opened the kitchen door, walked out, and slammed it shut.

Jessica tugged at Elizabeth's sleeve, and they both ran out into the kitchen. "What was that all about?" Jessica asked innocently.

May was peering through the window. "Steven just left," she said. "He said he was never coming back."

"Oh, don't worry," Elizabeth said. "He'll be back."

"I don't know." May craned her neck to look farther down the street. "He seemed pretty serious."

"Yeah, but you know Steven," Jessica said. "He'll be back for dinner."

May turned from the window and looked at Jessica. "Do you think so?" She looked pretty nervous.

"Sure," Jessica said.

"Of course," Elizabeth agreed. "Come on, Jess—I don't want to miss that German girl's skating routine."

She and Jessica went back into the living room and dropped onto the couch. Jessica poked Elizabeth in the ribs. "Isn't this great? It's working out just like I planned."

*   *   *

"I wonder where Steven is," Elizabeth said. She was in the kitchen, helping May set the table for dinner. It was nearly six o'clock.

"I hope he comes back soon," May said, looking out the kitchen window for what seemed like the hundredth time.

May was pacing back and forth so much that Elizabeth had to dodge her to get into the dining room to set the table. "Don't worry, May, Steven will be all right," she said on her way past.

"Oh, I don't know. I just don't know," May said.

Jessica poured herself a big glass of water and sat down at the kitchen table. "Maybe he went to a friend's house for dinner," she said. "Or he could have gone to a movie."

"But he took a bag with him," May said. "I think he really intended to run away."

Jessica drummed the table with her fingernails. "I hope not! Mom and Dad will be really upset if they get back, and he's not here."

May groaned. "Don't say that! He'll be back before the night's over. He has to be."

"Elizabeth, remember that other time that Steven ran away?" Jessica suddenly asked.

"What? What are you talking about?" May demanded.

"Well, a couple of months ago, Steven decided he wanted to live on his own, so he ran away from home and took a bus to Los Angeles," Jessica said.

Elizabeth couldn't believe her sister was making up such a big lie. May looked absolutely petrified!

"L-Los An-geles?" she stuttered.

"Of course, he came right back on the next bus," Jessica said. "But Mom and Dad sure were worried."

"He probably won't do something like that again," Elizabeth said.

"Probably? Oh, dear." May stopped pacing and looked out the window. "If anything happens to that boy, I'll never forgive myself."

"You know how teenagers are always doing weird things," Jessica said.

"Right," Elizabeth added.

Just then the phone rang, and May rushed to answer it. "Hello?" A look of relief swept over her face. "Steven, where are you?" She listened for a minute. "Yes," she said. "Yes, I understand. No, I'm not mad."

May covered the phone with her hand and said, "He's all right, girls. He's at a friend's house up in Palilla Canyon." Then she grabbed a pad of paper and a pen. "OK, Steven, go ahead." She jotted down several directions on the pad, then turned the paper over and continued writing. "It seems like quite a drive," she said when he was finished. "How long will it take? Are you sure? Fine. I'll be there as soon as I can. I'm leaving now. Good-bye, Steven. Now don't go anywhere."

May hung up the phone and ran to the hall closet.

"What's going on?" Jessica called after her.

"He got a ride to his friend's house, only his friend isn't there, so he's waiting at a convenience store nearby." She slipped her jacket over her shoulders. "I have to go pick him up."

"Should we come with you?" Jessica asked.

Elizabeth thought Jessica's suggestion was a little risky, considering the fact that May might just take her up on it!

"No, you girls wait here—eat your dinner. We'll be back soon." May grabbed her purse and the sheet of directions from the counter and car keys from the hook near the door. "Be careful! Don't let any strangers in!" she warned the twins on her way out.

"We won't!" Jessica replied. The door closed and she turned to Elizabeth. "We're only letting in friends!"

Ten

◇

"Anybody home?"

Jessica and Elizabeth ran into the kitchen from the living room, where they had been busy moving furniture out of the way.

"Steven, you're home!" Jessica cried, rushing toward him. "Oh, I thought I'd never see you again!" She threw her arms around his neck and hugged him.

Steven laughed and pulled her arms away. "Don't go overboard. Anyway, there's still a bunch of stuff outside we have to bring in."

"How did you get home?" asked Elizabeth.

"I took a cab—I had too much to carry. Palilla Canyon's a long way away, you know," he said, grinning.

"Yeah, and so's the supermarket," Jessica said.

"I can't believe she bought it," Steven said as they carried in the bags of soda, chips, and sandwich stuff from the driveway.

"I can," Jessica said. "It was a perfect plan."

"Modest, aren't you?" Steven asked, setting down a bag on the kitchen table. "I'm going upstairs to change while you guys finish getting everything ready."

"No fair!" Jessica cried. "Why do we have to do all the work?"

Steven walked over to the stairs. "Hey, I already did the hard part. I ran away from home and bought all the groceries. I need a break."

"OK, where should we put all this stuff?" Jessica asked Elizabeth.

"I'll get some bowls to put the chips and pretzels in," Elizabeth said. "Why don't you put the cups and ice on the card table?"

In the living room, Jessica popped one of her favorite CDs into the stereo and turned it up loud. She danced around the room as she arranged everything and brought out the food from the kitchen. Steven had taken care of everything on their list, including a deli platter of different cold cuts, pickles, carrots, and celery. They had onion dip and buns to make sandwiches with, too. Jessica put out jars of mustard, mayonnaise, and ketchup—she figured her parents would never miss those. Elizabeth popped several batches of popcorn and set them out in bowls around the living room.

It was almost seven, and Jessica couldn't wait for people to start showing up. She poured herself a cup of orange soda and stood in front of the mirror over the couch. "Do I look OK?" she asked Elizabeth. She shook her head to make her hair fall into place.

"You look great." Elizabeth wiped her hands on a napkin and looked around the living room. "This place looks great, too!"

"You told everyone to come at seven, right?"

Elizabeth nodded.

"Good. If people come too late, the party won't be over in time." Jessica didn't even want to think about what May would do to them if she got back and the party was still going. They planned on telling May that Steven got a ride home from his friend, who supposedly showed up at the convenience store after getting Steven's note. Steven was going to tell May that he was really bad at giving directions. Boy, is he ever, Jessica thought with a smile. But if May got back too soon . . .

Just then the doorbell rang, and Jessica practically jumped. "It's really happening!" She squeezed her sister's arm and ran to get the door.

Lila was standing outside, carrying a small

bag. "Hi," she said, walking into the kitchen. "Is anyone else here?"

"Not yet," Jessica said. "You're the first one."

"So, you're really going to pull this off," Lila said, wandering around the kitchen. "I can't believe it."

Jessica shrugged. "Sure, why not?" She was going to get in a little bragging about how independent she was when she spotted something on the refrigerator. "Uh, why don't you go put your CDs by the stereo," she said. "Elizabeth is in there. I'll be right in."

Lila walked into the living room, and Jessica hurried over to the refrigerator and removed May's long list of house rules. "Phew," she muttered. "That was a close one." Then she remembered something else she'd forgotten to do. She ran upstairs to May's room and quickly stuffed all of May's clothes and belongings under the bed.

Out in the hallway, Jessica ran into Steven. "Was that the door?" Steven asked.

"Lila's here," Jessica said.

"Oh. Well, tell me when some real people get here." Steven went back into his room, and Jessica stuck out her tongue at him.

When she got downstairs, the doorbell rang again. Jessica opened the door, and five of Steven's friends walked right past her into the house. "Where's Steven?" one of them asked.

"Upstairs," she said. "I'll get him." Jessica walked over to the stairs and yelled, "Steven! The real people are here!" Then she walked into the living room and grabbed a tortilla chip from one of the bowls. "OK, let's pick out something really good to play," she said to Lila and Elizabeth. "Before Steven's dumb friends try to take over!"

"Hi, Brooke," Elizabeth said. "I'm glad you're here. Come on in!"

"Thanks. Wow—there are a lot of people here," Brooke Dennis said as she walked into the living room.

"I know," Elizabeth said. "It's getting really crowded. Do you want something to drink?"

"Sure." Brooke followed Elizabeth to the card table. "I'll take a root beer, if that's OK."

"One root beer, coming up. So, did you hear when your mother's coming to visit yet?" Elizabeth poured the soda into a cup.

Brooke nodded and took a sip of root beer. "She called me today, actually."

"Really? What did she say?" Elizabeth asked. It was hard to talk with the music blasting so loudly.

"She's coming back next week." Brooke chewed the edge of her cup nervously.

"I bet you can't wait to see her," Elizabeth said, helping herself to a cup of soda.

"Actually, I'm kind of worried about it," Brooke replied. "She says she has a few surprises for me."

"Surprises are usually good, don't you think? Like surprise parties and surprise guests—stuff like that."

Brooke shrugged. "Maybe. I don't know. I haven't seen her in a long time, and I keep getting this weird feeling, like I'm not going to know her anymore or something."

"It must be hard to be separated from her," Elizabeth said. She couldn't imagine how she would feel if her parents ever got a divorce, like Brooke's had.

"It is," Brooke agreed. "But I am looking forward to seeing her, even if it does make me nervous."

"Hi, guys," Amy said, coming up behind them. "Brooke, I love your sweater."

"Hi, Amy. Thanks." Brooke smiled. "Wow, this place is packed."

"I know, isn't it great? So Amy, where's Rob?" Elizabeth asked.

"Over there, talking to Todd." Amy pointed to the far corner of the living room.

"Is that your new boyfriend?" Brooke asked.

"Sort of," Amy said.

"Sort of?" Elizabeth asked, trying not to sound too hopeful.

"Oh, he's definitely my boyfriend," Amy said quickly. "I was just going over there. Want to come with me?"

"I'm going to talk to Julie and Mary," Brooke said. "I'll catch you later."

"OK," Elizabeth said. "I haven't been able to talk to Todd all night, I've been so busy answering the door."

Todd and Rob were arguing about baseball when Amy and Elizabeth made their way through the crowd to them. Amy gently punched Rob on the arm. "Hi."

Rob turned and smiled at her. "Hi." Then he turned back to Todd. "I'm telling you, the record for the most stolen bases in one season is held by the same guy who had the most hits in one year."

"OK, OK, I believe you," Todd said. "Hi, Elizabeth. Hi, Amy."

"Hi, are you guys having a good time?" Elizabeth asked. She moved a little closer to Todd.

"Yeah, this is great. There must be a hundred people in here! How about you? Are you having fun?" Todd asked.

"Actually, I am," Elizabeth said. She couldn't get over how many people had come. Some people were dancing, others talking and eating, and everyone seemed to be having a good time. Practically the whole sixth grade was in her living room!

After living under May's rules all week, it felt great to have the house full of her friends.

"Hey, do you have any other food?" Rob asked.

"Everything's out," Elizabeth said. "There's stuff for sandwiches over there."

"You don't have any pizza?" Rob asked.

Elizabeth shook her head.

"What about ice cream?" Rob continued.

Elizabeth felt like pouring a bottle of soda on Rob's head. "Nope. No ice cream. Sorry."

"There's some cheese and crackers over by the couch," Amy said sweetly. "I'll get some for you." She walked away, leaving Elizabeth and Todd to talk to Rob. The longer Amy stayed away, the more Elizabeth suspected she had only offered to get the crackers because *she* didn't want to be with Rob, either.

"I can't stand this song," Rob said, frowning. "Don't you have any good music?"

"Go ahead, help yourself," Elizabeth offered. "Put on something else."

"OK, I will," Rob said. He walked over to the stereo, and Elizabeth sighed with relief.

"I thought he'd never leave," she said.

"I know," said Todd. "Now if only you could get him to leave the party. Look, Aaron's here— I'll be right back, OK?"

Elizabeth smiled. "Sure." She looked around the room. There were a lot of kids she didn't recognize, but they looked older, so she figured they were Steven's friends. She spotted Ken Matthews near the kitchen, talking to Tom McKay. As she watched Ken, she saw him looking over at Amy.

Amy came back over to Elizabeth. "Where's Rob?"

Elizabeth pointed to the stereo. Steven and Rob were in the middle of an argument about which music to put on next.

"Oh," Amy said. "You know what? I just walked past Janet Howell, and even *she* said she was having a good time. So you know your party is a total hit."

"Good," Elizabeth said, laughing. She didn't really care what Janet thought, but she knew Jessica did.

"Ken and Aaron and those guys seem to be having fun, too," Amy said, looking around the room.

"Amy, can I ask you something?"

"I know—I said I was going to get the cheese and crackers, and I didn't get any," Amy said with a laugh.

"No, it's not that." Elizabeth looked seriously at Amy. "I don't want to make you mad, but . . . do you really like Rob? I mean, he's not very nice."

Amy blushed. "He is kind of a jerk, isn't he?" she said. "You're right, Elizabeth. I don't really like him."

"Then how come you're going out with him?"

"I don't know. I mean, he seemed OK at first. He's cute and everything." Amy paused and looked at her sheepishly. "You know what, I guess I just wanted to have a boyfriend. That sounds silly, but I felt kind of worried when you started going out with Todd."

"Worried?" Elizabeth asked. "Why?"

Amy shrugged. "Because you had a boyfriend, and I didn't. I've been worried you're going to start doing everything with Todd instead of me. I thought maybe if I had a boyfriend then the four of us could do things together."

"Not if the boyfriend is Rob," Elizabeth said, rolling her eyes. "Seriously, though, I'm not going to stop doing stuff with you just because I go out with Todd. You're still my best friend. That's not going to change."

"Really?" Amy asked.

"Really," Elizabeth said.

Amy and Elizabeth glanced over at Rob, who was still arguing with Steven. "Now there's only one problem. How do I get rid of Rob?"

"I guess you can't tonight," Elizabeth said. "I mean, he's your date and everything. Just don't go out with him again. You deserve a lot better than him, you know." She nudged Amy with her elbow. "And I happen to know that a certain someone has been staring at you all night."

"Like who?" Amy said.

Elizabeth smiled. "I'll give you a hint. His initials are KM."

Just then Elizabeth heard the telephone ring over the din of the party. "I'll get it!" she cried, running into the kitchen.

Elizabeth grabbed the phone at the same time as Jessica. "I've got it," Jessica said. "Hello?" she said. "Oh, hi, May, how are you?"

Elizabeth ran into the living room and turned down the stereo. "It's just for a second," she told the crowd that was now spilling onto the patio. Then she hurried back into the kitchen.

"You're where?" Jessica asked. "Uh-huh, right. Well, I don't know, I've never been there. No, he hasn't called here. I'm sure he's OK, though. It's not that late yet."

Elizabeth glanced at the clock on the wall. It was already nine-fifteen! May had been gone for almost three hours. She was probably worried sick. And she'd been driving around lost in the dark, all by herself. *Maybe it was time to tell her what was really going on*, Elizabeth thought.

"What noise?" Jessica said. "Oh, you mean those voices? That's the TV. We can't sleep, we're too upset."

Elizabeth was about to grab the phone and tell May that Steven was home safe when Jessica said, "OK, we'll see you later!" and hung up the phone.

"Did she sound really worried?" Elizabeth asked.

Jessica shrugged. "She sounded OK. She's still following Steven's directions, only she hasn't found the store yet. She said she's about two hours away from Sweet Valley."

"I feel kind of bad for her," Elizabeth said. "Don't you?"

"Yeah, but I'm having too much—yuck!" Jessica lifted her foot off the floor. Her shoe was covered with grape soda.

Someone in the living room turned the stereo back up—about three times louder than it had been before. The walls were shaking from the noise. "I hope the neighbors can't hear this!" Elizabeth said.

"Hey, get out of there!" Jessica yelled at a boy who was taking a package of cookies out of the cupboard.

He ignored her and took the bag into the living room.

Elizabeth looked around the kitchen. It was a total mess. There were half-full cups everywhere, and popcorn was sprinkled on the floor like confetti. She heard a loud whoop from upstairs and three guys she didn't know came running down into the kitchen, laughing.

"You're not supposed to go upstairs!" Jessica said, still trying to clean off her shoe with a paper towel.

"Who are you, my mother?" one of the guys said. He opened the refrigerator and grabbed a jar of pickles.

"Hey!" Jessica cried.

But the boys had already disappeared into the crowd.

Elizabeth picked up a cup from the floor and tossed it into the trash. "Jess, do you think maybe things are getting a little out of control?"

Elizabeth didn't hear Jessica's answer—it was drowned out by a loud crash from the living room.

Eleven

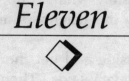

"It was only a lamp," Steven told Elizabeth when she rushed into the room. "It didn't break."

Elizabeth looked at the lamp lying next to the couch. It still worked, and it didn't seem bent. "That was close," she said.

"I know," Steven said. He looked a little nervous. "Uh, there are a lot of people here, aren't there?"

Elizabeth went over to the stereo and turned the volume down. "Can everyone please try to be careful from now on?" she asked the crowd. "We really don't want anything to get broken."

"I thought there weren't any parents here!" someone yelled.

"There aren't. It's just that—" Elizabeth was interrupted by a loud blast of music. She turned around and saw Rob with his hand on the volume knob.

"Lighten up and have some fun!" he yelled to Elizabeth.

She shook her head and walked over to Steven. "I don't know what to do," she said. "If it stays this loud, the neighbors are going to complain."

"I'll go outside and get the people out there to come in," Steven said. "Then we can lock the sliding glass door."

"I'll come with you," Elizabeth said.

She and Steven walked out onto the patio. There were at least twenty people in the yard and around the pool.

"Do you know any of these people?" Elizabeth asked.

Steven shook his head. "I've never even seen them before."

"Where did they come from?"

"Beats me," Steven said. He tapped a girl on the shoulder. "Excuse me, but would you mind going inside? We're trying to keep the noise down."

She turned to face him. "Are you saying I'm loud?"

"No, it's just that the neighbors are going to complain," Steven said. "We have to do something."

"So let them complain," the girl said.

"Come on, let's go inside," her friend said. "I want to get some more food anyway."

Elizabeth and Steven walked over to talk to the next group of people, but Elizabeth stopped when she saw the pool. She couldn't believe her eyes. Plastic cups, cardboard plates, potato chips, pretzels, and practically every other imaginable thing were floating around. It looked like a big bowl of soup! "Steven, look at the pool," she finally managed to say.

"Oh, great," Steven grumbled. "That should only take about two hours to clean."

"We'd better get started now," Elizabeth said.

Steven sighed. "Why did I let Jessica talk me into this party?" Then he got down on his hands and knees and started picking things out of the pool. Elizabeth got a trash can from the patio and brought it over.

Elizabeth had just gotten the last group of people to go inside when she heard a loud splash. "Agh!" Steven cried. Elizabeth turned around and saw Steven floating in the pool amid the garbage. Some boys were standing on the patio, laughing.

"Get lost," Steven yelled to them, "before I make you!"

"Oh, we're so scared!" one of them yelled back. Then they disappeared into the house.

Steven got out of the pool and wrung out his shirt. "I think I'll go change," he muttered. Elizabeth could hear the water squishing in his sneakers as he walked over to the patio. A few seconds after he walked into the living room, Elizabeth heard loud laughter.

Poor Steven, she thought as she pulled more of the litter out of the pool.

"Jessica, I have to get going," Aaron said. "I told my parents I'd be home by ten-thirty."

"Really? Do you have to go? We've hardly seen each other at all."

"I know," Aaron said. "It's been pretty crowded."

"Do you think everyone's having fun?" Jessica asked.

"Yeah, this was a really good party." Aaron looked around the room. "I wonder how late people are going to stay."

"Not too late, I hope," Jessica said.

"When are your parents coming home?" Aaron asked.

"Tomorrow, around noon."

"Good luck getting this place cleaned up," Aaron picked a cup off the floor and put it in the wastebasket.

"Thanks, we'll need it!" Jessica said with a laugh.

"Well, thanks for inviting me," Aaron said. "I'd better go. A bunch of us are walking home together."

"Oh," Jessica said, feeling disappointed. "Well, thanks for coming. It wouldn't have been a party without you."

Aaron smiled. "I had a great time." Then he took a few steps closer.

Jessica's heart started beating faster. She couldn't believe it. Everything was turning out just like she planned—Aaron was going to kiss her! And in front of everybody! He really did like her!

Aaron leaned down and kissed Jessica lightly on the lips. She felt all tingly inside. It was better than she'd ever imagined, it was fantastic, it was—

"Smack!"

Jessica jumped back from Aaron and touched her face. A piece of bologna had just come flying through the air and hit her on the cheek.

Everyone around them burst out laughing.

"Who did that?" Aaron said.

"I don't know, but whoever it was, they're leaving. *Now*." Jessica shouted. She felt her face turn bright red.

Another cold cut went flying across the room and hit the window. It stuck there. Then somebody cried, "Food fight!"

Within thirty seconds, food was flying all over the Wakefield living room.

"That was the funniest thing I've ever seen," Lila said, giggling hysterically as she ducked down next to Jessica. "You should have seen the look on your face when that piece of bologna hit you! I wish I had my video camera." She burst out laughing all over again.

Jessica frowned at her. "Very funny." She stood up and walked away, through the flying pieces of bologna and popcorn. Anything was better than listening to Lila make fun of her first kiss!

A glob of mustard hit Jessica on the neck as she ran over, grabbed the deli platter, and brought it into the kitchen. Elizabeth was already there, hiding the onion dip. She had a red sticky glob of ketchup in her hair, and tortilla chips stuck to her sweater. Jessica was so angry, she couldn't even laugh.

"I don't believe this," Steven said, carrying in the rest of the food. They were hurriedly throwing everything they could into big green garbage bags as a stream of people came through the kitchen.

"See you later, Jess!" Lila called, as she and the rest of the Unicorns went out the door. Aaron followed them, and so did most of her and Elizabeth's other friends.

"Sorry, I can't stay and help," Brooke said. "I told my dad I'd be home ten minutes ago."

"See you later," Aaron called.

"I can't believe they all just left," Jessica muttered, wiping her neck with a paper towel.

"Maybe everyone else will take the hint and leave now, too," Steven grumbled. His hair was still soaking wet from the pool.

When they finished disposing of all the food and cleaned themselves off, they walked back into the living room. "This place is trashed," Jessica observed dismally.

"Yeah, and the only people I know here are Todd, Ken, and Amy," Elizabeth said. "Who are those other people?"

"I don't know, but they'd better leave soon," Jessica complained. "They're the ones who started the food fight."

Elizabeth peeled a slice of ham off a lamp. "It's getting pretty late—it's almost eleven. They have to go soon."

"Look at that jerk over by the stereo," Steven said. "He keeps changing the music every five seconds."

"That's Amy's new boyfriend," Elizabeth said. "Or was, anyway."

"I'm going to put on something really mellow, like one of Mom's tapes," Jessica said. "Then maybe people will—hey! He just took my CDs!"

Jessica marched over to the stereo, but Ken

was already there. "I saw you take those," Ken said. "Give them back."

"I didn't take anything," Rob said.

"I saw you, too," Jessica said, her arms folded across her chest.

"I can't believe this. I'm just standing here, trying to play good music so everyone has a good time, and you come over and accuse me of stealing."

Ken grabbed a jean jacket that was lying on the floor next to Rob and four discs fell out. "Are these yours?"

"No, they're mine!" Jessica said. "I always write my name on the inside of the case. Go ahead, check them."

Ken opened up one of the disc cases and showed the name to Rob. "Are you Jessica Wakefield?"

"No—lucky for me, I'm not!" Rob replied with a laugh. He looked at Amy and smiled, but she didn't respond.

"Why don't you leave," Ken said. "Now."

"Sure," Rob said, grabbing his jacket. "Come on, Amy, let's go. This was a lame party anyway."

"No, thanks," Amy said. "I'm staying." She looked at Ken, who smiled at her.

"OK, fine. I'll call you," Rob said, heading for the door.

"Don't bother!" Amy called after him.

"What a jerk," Jessica said. "Thanks for getting my CDs back for me, Ken."

"No problem," Ken said. "Listen, I should get going pretty soon myself."

"Oh, um, Ken, do you feel like walking home with me?" Amy asked.

"Sure," Ken said. "I mean, it's on the way and everything."

Elizabeth smiled at Amy as she walked by.

"I guess things look good between Ken and Amy," Todd said when they were gone. "I'd better go, too." He looked around the living room. "Are you guys going to be all right?"

"Yeah, we're going to get Steven to kick out all his friends now so we can clean up," Jessica said.

"We hope so, anyway," Elizabeth added.

"OK, well, be careful," Todd said. "Call me tomorrow and let me know how it goes with your parents." Elizabeth walked him to the door.

Jessica found Steven talking to a pretty girl over in the corner. "Come on, Steven, tell all your friends to leave," she said. "We have to clean up!"

"All my friends?" Steven said. "I don't know any of these people. Except for Tiffany here."

All of a sudden, the speakers were blasting heavy metal music again. "Let's rock and roll!" a boy wearing a leather jacket yelled. He stood up on the coffee table and started dancing. A minute later, everyone was standing on the furniture, dancing.

"Come on, you guys, you have to leave!" Jessica cried.

"Leave? The party's just getting started!" a girl shouted back.

Jessica glanced at the ceiling, where a scoop of macaroni salad threatened to fall onto her head at any second. "What are we going to do?" she wailed.

"Emergency conference in the kitchen!" Steven said, grabbing her by the arm. On their way, he turned down the stereo, but someone turned it right back up again.

"We have to get these people out of our house, and fast!" Steven said.

"I know, but how?" Elizabeth asked.

The kitchen door started to open, and Jessica groaned.

"The party's over—don't come in!" Steven yelled.

The door swung open anyway. May was standing there, glaring at them. "I was just leaving," she said frostily and left the room without another word.

Twelve

Elizabeth knocked on the door. "Can we come in?" There was no answer. She looked at Jessica and shrugged. They slowly pushed the door open and walked into the master bedroom.

May was pulling her clothes out from underneath the bed and stuffing them into her suitcase. She didn't look up.

"Where are you going?" Jessica asked.

"Home!" May said sharply.

"May, we're sorry," Elizabeth said. "We're really, really sorry."

"Yeah, we feel terrible about tricking you that way," Jessica added.

"I bet you do," May said as she dumped her shoes into the suitcase.

"We should never have tried to have this party," Elizabeth said. "We made a terrible mistake. The house is a disaster, and there are all these people here we don't know."

"You can't leave," Jessica said. "We need your help!"

May didn't say anything.

"May, I wanted to tell you Steven was OK," Elizabeth said. "We didn't mean to make you so worried. It's just that we got carried away."

"We shouldn't have made you drive all over California," Jessica added. "If you'd been here, things never would have gotten so crazy. Please say you'll help us. These people won't leave!"

May looked at them angrily. "You've gotten yourselves into this mess. Now, go away and let me pack!"

Jessica and Elizabeth walked back into the hall. "What should we do?" Jessica asked.

Suddenly, there was another loud crash downstairs. "What now," Jessica muttered as they hurried to the stairs.

"I hope it's not a window," Elizabeth said.

Steven met them at the bottom of the stairs. "One of Dad's diplomas just fell off the wall in the den. The glass broke, but the diploma's OK." He opened the broom closet and took out a small broom and a dustpan. "What did May say?"

"Nothing," Jessica said glumly. "She's leaving."

"Mom and Dad are going to kill us," Jessica

said. The music was still blaring in the living room as she, Steven, and Jessica went into the den to clean up the broken glass. '

Elizabeth was smoothing out her father's diploma on the desk when she heard a familiar sound.

"Is that what I think it is?"

They all ran out to the front hall. There was May, blowing her whistle as loudly as ever. She blew it five times, then walked over to the stereo and shut it off. "I want everybody out of here immediately!" she announced. "That means now!"

A boy jumped off the couch and walked over to her. "Where did you come from?" he mumbled, picking up his jacket.

"Good night, young man," May said sternly. She blew the whistle again. "Come on, get a move on!" she yelled to the remaining guests.

"Are you for real?" a girl said.

May walked over and stood in front of the girl, giving her a deadly stare. "OK, I'm going," the girl said.

Elizabeth had to hand it to May. She was pretty intimidating. Within five minutes, the house was completely empty—of people, anyway. It was absolutely full of garbage. "Thank you so much, May," she said.

"Yeah, you saved us," Jessica said. "Those kids were awful."

May stared around her at the mess. "Maybe I should have made them pick up before they left!"

"That's OK, they probably would have started another food fight," Steven said.

"Is that how this happened?" May shook her head. "I have never in all my years seen a house in such bad shape."

"Uh, May, I didn't get a chance to tell you before, but I want to apologize," Steven said, staring at the carpet. "We shouldn't have tried to fool you like that. I guess you hate us now, if you didn't already."

"I don't hate you," May said. "I don't especially like you right now, but—"

"It's just that, see, our parents didn't tell us we were going to have a baby-sitter," Steven hurried to explain. "We thought we were going to be on our own, so we planned this party. Then they told us you were coming, and, well, we were kind of mad about it."

"Mad enough to put tabasco sauce in a pot of coffee?" May asked.

"Yeah," Steven admitted. "Sorry about that."

"I'm sorry, too," Elizabeth said. "I guess we were pretty mad at our parents, only we took it out on you."

"Well, I don't know." May cleared a spot on the couch and sat down. "I had a lot of time to think tonight, while I drove all over the state of

California. On my way back here, I was trying to figure out why you'd pull such a stunt. I realize I made a lot of rules, and I was very strict with you. You see, I never had to look after older children before. And even though I know you're more responsible about some things, I also know it's easier to get into bigger trouble when you're older. I've never had children of my own, but I've seen friends try to handle their teenagers. It looked so difficult. I thought I'd better keep you on your toes right from the start. I wanted to make sure you'd be here, safe and sound, when your parents got back."

"And that's why you made us eat peas and spinach all the time?" asked Jessica.

May laughed. Elizabeth almost fell over—it was the first time she had heard May laugh! "Actually, that's one thing I do believe in—eating lots of vegetables," May said. "I guess I pushed it a little too much, eh?"

"Just a little," Elizabeth said, wrinkling her nose.

"Well, I'll accept your apology if you'll accept mine," May offered. "And now, we have some work to do!" She got up from the couch and surveyed the room. "We need to clean the walls, the rugs, the—"

"Listen, May," Elizabeth said. "If you really accept our apology you have to promise us one thing: that you will not lift a finger to clean up this mess. It's our fault.''

Steven and Jessica nodded.

May looked at each one of them. "I guess you haven't been brought up so badly after all.''

Early the next morning, Jessica, Elizabeth, and Steven tiptoed out of their rooms and down the stairs.

"Shhhhh,'' Elizabeth said. "May is still asleep.''

"Can you believe we're getting up at five-thirty by choice?'' Jessica whispered.

"What do you mean by choice?'' Steven whispered back. "Mom and Dad are going to be home by noon and the house looks like a tornado hit it.''

They headed to the broom closet for supplies. Steven handed Jessica a bucket and a bottle of cleaner. "You do the walls,'' he said. He handed a big green garbage bag to Elizabeth. "You start picking up garbage. I'll wash the kitchen floor,'' he said.

After several hours of furious cleaning, Elizabeth had to admit the house looked pretty good. In fact it was so clean, it looked even better than it had when her parents left. The only thing they would have to explain was the broken diploma frame, but that wasn't too serious. With Steven and his basketball around, that kind of thing happened all the time.

But there was something else they were going to have to explain—the wooden rose—and Elizabeth really wasn't looking forward to it.

"The house is so clean I can't believe it," Jessica said, collapsing on the sofa next to her.

"Pretty good timing, too," Elizabeth said. "Mom and Dad will be home in an hour."

Steven flipped off the vacuum. "Do you think May is going to tell them about last night?"

"I really hope not," Jessica said. "Where is May, anyway? She's been gone for hours."

"I don't know," Elizabeth said. "She said she had some errands to do."

A few minutes later, the door opened and May walked in. "Hello!" she said cheerfully. She handed a small brown bag to Elizabeth.

"What is it?" she asked. "Breakfast?"

"Just open it," May urged.

Elizabeth unfolded the top of the bag and peered inside. "It's the rose!" she cried. "How did you find it? How did you even know it was missing?"

"Well, it's kind of a long story," May said. "Remember that day we got into a big fight because you came home late?"

Elizabeth nodded.

"I was running some errands at that mini-mall downtown, near the Valley Mall, and I saw you come out of Valley Antiques," May explained.

"You did?" Elizabeth said.

May nodded. "That's why when I asked where you'd been, and you said school, I got upset. I knew you were lying to me."

"Sorry," Elizabeth said.

"That's in the past," May said. "Anyway, I didn't know why you were there, but this morning, I got a call from the owner of that shop. He said that he was at an auction in Big Mesa, and he'd seen what he thought was your antique rose on display. So I went up there, and he told me the whole story. Then I met the man who was selling it. He's a professional antique dealer," May said. "He spends a lot of time at garage sales, looking for items that people don't realize are valuable. So I asked him a lot of questions, such as, did he buy it from a girl with blond hair on Thursday," May explained.

"Did he give it back to you?" Jessica asked.

"Not exactly," May said. She took off her hat and placed it on the table.

"What do you mean, not exactly?" Elizabeth asked.

"He was selling it for two hundred dollars," May said.

Elizabeth was stunned. "You paid two hundred dollars for this?"

May shook her head.

"You mean the bidding went even higher?" Steven asked.

"It could have," May said. "But I talked the man down to fifty dollars."

"You're kidding!" Jessica said. "How did you do that? He paid seventy-five!"

"Oh, I can be pretty tough when I want to be," May said with a wink.

Everybody laughed, even May.

Elizabeth heard the sound of tires in the driveway, and she jumped up. "They're here!"

May grabbed her hat and pulled it back over her purplish-gray hair. Elizabeth looked at her sister hopefully.

Elizabeth ran out the door to greet her parents, with Steven, Jessica, and May right behind her. "Welcome back!" she cried.

"It's so good to see you!" Mrs. Wakefield said, hugging Elizabeth tightly.

"Did you miss us?" Mr. Wakefield said, wrapping his arms around Jessica.

"Maybe just a little," she replied. Then she kissed him on the cheek.

Mr. Wakefield turned to May. "So, was it everything you expected?"

"Yes and no," May said.

"Were the kids any trouble?" Mrs. Wakefield asked.

Jessica, Elizabeth, and Steven all turned and looked nervously at May.

"Nothing I couldn't handle," May replied, smiling. Jessica, Elizabeth, and Steven smiled, too.

"That's good to hear, not that I'm at all surprised." Mr. Wakefield opened the trunk. "I'd better get these bags in the house."

"I'll help," Mrs. Wakefield said.

"Well, I guess I might as well get going," May said.

"You're leaving already?" Steven asked. He walked over toward her, and so did the twins.

"I have things I need to do at home. I thought you'd be glad to get rid of me," May said.

"Wait right there," Jessica said. She ran into the house.

"Thank you so much for everything, May," Elizabeth said. "And especially for finding the rose. You don't know how much that means to me."

"Oh, I think I do," May said. She leaned forward and hugged Elizabeth. "I'm glad I could help."

"Well, uh, make sure you have a safe trip home," Steven said. "Don't take any wrong turns."

May smiled. "I won't."

Jessica came running out the door with a large piece of paper in her hand. She handed it to May.

"Official Honorary Grandmother Certificate,"

May read out loud. "This is so sweet!" She looked like she was going to cry, but then she turned to Jessica and said, "Honorary has two r's, not three." She laughed and hugged Jessica. She walked over to her car, which was parked in the street. "Good-bye! Tell your parents I'll be in touch. I'll stop in and see you sometime!"

"Bye!" the three of them yelled.

"You know, I can't believe I'm saying this, but I think I'm actually going to miss her," Steven said as they walked back up to the house.

"When you get up tomorrow at seven-fifteen, you mean?" Elizabeth teased him.

"When you come home from school and eat nine cookies in a row?" Jessica said, opening the door.

"Well, I guess I'll get over it," Steven said.

When Jessica and Elizabeth arrived at school on Monday morning, a big crowd of people was waiting for them.

"Great party!" Ken Matthews called out as they walked past.

"Yeah, when's the next one?" Tom McKay added.

"Never," Elizabeth whispered out of the corner of her mouth, and Jessica giggled. They walked over to where a group of their friends was standing.

"Hi, you guys!" Mary Wallace said. "Did you get everything cleaned up before your parents got home?"

Elizabeth smiled. "It was nothing."

"When did they get back?" asked Amy.

"Around noon," Jessica said.

"Did they suspect anything?" Lila asked.

"No, of course not," Jessica said nonchalantly.

"That was a great party," Amy said. "I mean, until the food fight. Even that was kind of fun."

"Everyone's talking about it," Mary said. "I think the whole school was there."

Jessica looked triumphantly at Lila.

Brooke Dennis walked over to join the group. "Hi, everyone," she said. "Thanks for the fun party Saturday night, you guys."

"Sure," Elizabeth said. "Thanks for coming."

"Guess what, Elizabeth?" Brooke said. "I talked to my mother yesterday. She's in New York!"

"Really?" Lila asked. "I thought she lived in Paris."

"She does," Brooke said. "But she's coming out to visit me. She'll be here on Thursday."

"How long has it been since you've seen her?" Jessica asked.

"About six months," Brooke said. "I haven't even met my new half-sister, Sonya. She's already a year old—I can't believe it."

"I bet you can't wait," Elizabeth said.

Brooke smiled nervously. "I can't. It seems like forever until Thursday."

"Why is she in New York? Why isn't she here now?" Lila asked.

"She said she had some business to take care of." Brooke shrugged. "Whatever that means."

"Have you found out what her surprise is yet?" Elizabeth asked.

"Nope. She mentioned it again, though," Brooke said.

"It must be something really big," Elizabeth said.

"Maybe you're going to have another half-sister," Jessica guessed. "Or half-brother."

"I don't know," Brooke said. "But whatever it is, I'll find out soon!"

What is Brooke's mother's big surprise? Find out in Sweet Valley Twins #55, **BROOKE AND HER ROCK-STAR MOM.**

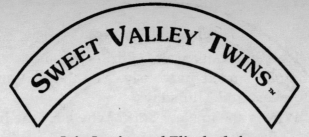

Join Jessica and Elizabeth for
big adventure in exciting
SWEET VALLEY TWINS SUPER EDITIONS
and SWEET VALLEY TWINS CHILLERS.

☐ **#1: CLASS TRIP**   15588-1/$3.50
☐ **#2: HOLIDAY MISCHIEF**   15641-1/$3.50
☐ **#3: THE BIG CAMP SECRET**   15707-8/$3.50
☐ **SWEET VALLEY TWINS SUPER SUMMER
FUN BOOK by Laurie Pascal Wenk**
                    15816-3/$3.50/3.95
Elizabeth shares her favorite summer projects &
Jessica gives you pointers on parties. Plus:
fashion tips, space to record your favorite
summer activities, quizzes, puzzles, a summer
calendar, photo album, scrapbook, address book
& more!

CHILLERS

☐ **#1: THE CHRISTMAS GHOST   15767-1/$3.50**
☐ **#2: THE GHOST IN THE GRAVEYARD**
                    15801-5/$3.50
☐ **#3: THE CARNIVAL GHOST   15859-7/$2.95**

Bantam Books, Dept. SVT6, 414 East Golf Road, Des Plaines, IL 60016

Please send me the items I have checked above. I am enclosing $_____
(please add $2.50 to cover postage and handling). Send check or money
order, no cash or C.O.D.s please.

Mr/Ms _____

Address _____

City/State _____ Zip _____

SVT6-9/91

Please allow four to six weeks for delivery.
Prices and availability subject to change without notice.

SWEET VALLEY TWINS ™

☐	15681-0	**TEAMWORK #27**	**$2.75**
☐	15688-8	**APRIL FOOL! #28**	**$2.75**
☐	15695-0	**JESSICA AND THE BRAT ATTACK #29**	**$2.75**
☐	15715-9	**PRINCESS ELIZABETH #30**	**$2.95**
☐	15727-2	**JESSICA'S BAD IDEA #31**	**$2.75**
☐	15747-7	**JESSICA ON STAGE #32**	**$2.99**
☐	15753-1	**ELIZABETH'S NEW HERO #33**	**$2.99**
☐	15766-3	**JESSICA, THE ROCK STAR #34**	**$2.99**
☐	15772-8	**AMY'S PEN PAL #35**	**$2.95**
☐	15778-7	**MARY IS MISSING #36**	**$2.99**
☐	15779-5	**THE WAR BETWEEN THE TWINS #37**	**$2.99**
☐	15789-2	**LOIS STRIKES BACK #38**	**$2.99**
☐	15798-1	**JESSICA AND THE MONEY MIX-UP #39**	**$2.95**
☐	15806-6	**DANNY MEANS TROUBLE #40**	**$2.99**
☐	15810-4	**THE TWINS GET CAUGHT #41**	**$2.99**
☐	15824-4	**JESSICA'S SECRET #42**	**$2.95**
☐	15835-X	**ELIZABETH'S FIRST KISS #43**	**$2.95**
☐	15837-6	**AMY MOVES IN #44**	**$2.95**
☐	15843-0	**LUCY TAKES THE REINS #45**	**$2.99**
☐	15849-X	**MADEMOISELLE JESSICA #46**	**$2.95**
☐	15869-4	**JESSICA'S NEW LOOK #47**	**$2.95**
☐	15880-5	**MANDY MILLER FIGHTS BACK #48**	**$2.99**
☐	15899-6	**THE TWINS' LITTLE SISTER #49**	**$2.99**
☐	15911-9	**JESSICA AND THE SECRET STAR #50**	**$2.99**

Bantam Books, Dept. SVT5, 414 East Golf Road, Des Plaines, IL 60016

Please send me the items I have checked above. I am enclosing $_____ (please add $2.50 to cover postage and handling). Send check or money order, no cash or C.O.D.s please.

Mr/Ms _____

Address _____

City/State _____ Zip _____

SVT5-9/91

Please allow four to six weeks for delivery.
Prices and availability subject to change without notice.

The most exciting story ever
in Sweet Valley history

FRANCINE
PASCAL'S
SWEET
VALLEY
Saga

THE SWEET VALLEY SAGA tells the incredible story of the lives and times of five generations of brave and beautiful young women who were Jessica and Elizabeth's ancestors. Their story is the story of America: from the danger of the pioneering days to the glamour of the roaring nineties, the sacrifice and romance of World War II to the rebelliousness of the Sixties, right up to the present-day Sweet Valley. A dazzling novel of unforgettable lives and love both lost and won, THE SWEET VALLEY SAGA is Francine Pascal's most memorable, exciting, and wonderful Sweet Valley book ever.

BANTAM
NEW YORK • TORONTO • LONDON • SYDNEY • AUCKLAND

AN 251 9/91